Fury Street

Fury Street

JACK REASON

A Black Horse Western

ROBERT HALE · LONDON

ISBN 0 7090 6499 3

Robert Hale Limited
Clerkenwell House
Clerkenwell Green
London EC1R 0HT

Photoset in North Wales by
Derek Doyle & Associates, Mold, Flintshire.
Printed and bound in Great Britain by
WBC Book Manufacturers Limited, Bridgend.

For M and R
in appreciation of their interest

One

It was just that, the hell-bent fury of it all on a
night when even the moon dripped blood, that
ripped the heart from the mid-west town of
Grateful and left it for dead. They never got to the
body count till sun-up.

Maybe they should have seen it coming; maybe
it had been there all along, nesting like a rattler
in the dark of memory, simply waiting for the
spark to unleash mayhem. Maybe they had
always known there would come just such a night.
Could be it had only ever been a matter of time.

Some had already figured it for that long back.
Sam McAndrew for one.

Sam had been with Grateful as sheriff for close
on ten years and seen most of what a one-time
trail town could throw up: the hopeless drifters,
lead-belly gunslingers, slick-spit gamblers, sales-
men, two-bit preachers, sod-busters, cattle kings,
cowboys and whores. Most, in fact, of the good and
the bottomed-out that flowed with the tide
through those years in the great drift West.

But the O'Mara boys had been different from

the start, minute they had ridden in at noon on that hot, dust-shrouded day.

Sam had spotted it straight out – lean, mean, silent men, down on their luck, hungry and deprived, all set to take whatever would ease aching bellies and calm troubled minds. No telling how far the four of them had come, from where or from what. No telling either how far they planned to go. Only reckoning Sam had resolved at that first sight was that Grateful was not far enough.

It had taken just a half-hour for the trouble to erupt.

A bar girl over at Shelley's Saloon in no mood to get passed from one set of filthy hands to the next, a spilled bottle of stale mescal, raised voices, somebody bolder, or drunker, than the rest chancing his hand against his better sense, cursed threats, the girl's dress torn from her, tables overturned, glasses smashed, guns drawn, four shots. . . .

And it was done.

One of the O'Mara boys lay dead in a thickening pool of blood and three were riding clear, deep into the barren lands of dirt and rocks and rattlers to the north. But not before one of them had shouted a warning to the crowded street.

'That's my brother yuh shot there. Yuh hear me? My brother! Sure as hell's teeth yuh'll pay for that, every last one, and yuh flea-bag town along of yuh. Yuh hear me, damn yuh? We'll be back! We'll be back!'

And that, as Sam McAndrew came to reflect long after, was how fury and the fear that would come to stand in its shadow and lead to that fateful night, first took root in the town of Grateful.

It had been only hours after the shooting at Shelley's that a handful of the town elders and businessmen had met in the back room at the saloon to, as storekeeper Ed Murtrey put it, 'reckon out' the shouted threat.

'Mebbe it was all noise,' he had said when the gathering were finally seated, the whiskey poured and the cigars glowing comfortably. 'Hell, fella gets to mouthin' wild when a shootin's done, 'specially when the body's one of yuh kind – yuh brother as it happens. But, well . . . that's all fire, ain't it, not for blazin' on? Come the cold light—'

'Cold light wouldn't change nothin' if it were me,' blacksmith Gus Coles had grunted. 'Blood kind is blood kind. Family, ain't it? Family doin' eats at a fella. I know, I seen it.'

'Yes, yes,' banker Charlie Catches had fluttered, tugging his fancy waistcoat over the roll of his paunch, 'that's all very well, but, damn it, these men, these scum, they don't react and respond same as the likes of you and me. Their kind ain't human, are they? Nothin' close. Stringin' t'gether more than a half-dozen words to make any sorta sense would be stretchin' vermin like that. As for emotion, anythin' remotely resemblin' remorse or feelin's for their kith and kin, why, I doubt if they've ever been troubled by more than a gut ache in their whole lives. It's all kill, be killed in their world; grab what yuh can, where yuh can and to hell with it. T'morrow don't exist. Revenge

talk is just that – all talk. No, we won't be hearin'
from them boys again. Take my word on it.'

'But you weren't there, were yuh? You didn't
see.' Nate Simpler's words had been whispered in
the same soft tones he would use to ask a fellow if
it was just a shave he wanted or had he the extra
for a bath.

'Well, no, as it happens I wasn't,' Charlie had
said, fidgeting his fingers over mother-of-pearl
buttons, 'but I don't see as how—'

'Yuh didn't see the look in them fellas' eyes, did
yuh? Yuh didn't see the hate, Charlie Catches. But
I sure as hell did. Oh, yes, I seen it, and I'm telling
yuh—'

'I didn't see nothin' of nothin',' said rooming-
house proprietor Walt Pond, his eyes round, arms
spread. 'Damn it, I wasn't even *in* town. Out there
at the Flankey homestead buyin' a horse. So who
shot who, f'Crissake? Who were these fellas?'

'Evil incarnate,' groaned Orton Grey, his
hooded, undertaker's eyes lowered to the swirling
dregs of his drink. 'Dark men moving through the
mists of Hell. Godforsaken and lost. Oh, yes, evil
incarnate, my friends.' He paused and sighed.
'Frank Gallons did well to rid this world of one of
'em. He had an edge there, yuh know. Real sharp.
One shot. Saved that poor gal from the carnage of
the flesh. Oh, yes.'

'The hell he had an edge!' snapped Gus Coles.
'Gallons was drunk – *again* – same as he always
is. Weren't no need to draw on them fellas. Gal
like Poll can take care of herself. Damnit, she's
been doin' it long enough! Frank Gallons was

booze-whipped, and he got lucky.'

'And makin' the most of it right now, right this minute out there in the bar,' said Murtrey, clamping his teeth on his cigar. 'Yuh heard him? Tellin' all and sundry as how he took out a *real* gunslinger. And men soakin' him fit to sink him for the tellin'.' He blew thick, angry smoke. 'Goin' to have to watch him. Could get outa hand.'

'Now, now,' gestured Charlie Catches, resting his empty glass against his paunch, 'it's *us* that's gettin' outa hand. Buildin' this into somethin' it ain't. So what we got, eh? What we *really* got? I'll tell yuh what we got. We got four men ridin' into town – scumbags I'll grant yuh, no question – and we got them same four trouble-rousin' straight off, lookin' for it, baitin' for it. Damn it, *wanting* it. Well, they sure as hell got it, and t'ain't no use layin' blame for the shootin' at Frank Gallons's door. He did what any man with a streak of decency about him would've done. Sure he did, drunk or not, and I for one—'

'Dark men cast long shadows. They'll be back,' croaked Grey, finishing his drink in one gulp. 'There'll be some pine parties top of Boot Hill, yuh bet there will. Oh, yes, yuh can bet.'

'That's it, ain't it?' said Murtrey. 'That's the whole of it. *Will they be back?*'

' 'Course they will,' drawled Coles.

'Seen it in their eyes,' murmured Simpler.

'That's fool talk,' began Catches.

'Just who's *they*?' said Pond, slapping the table. 'Will somebody please tell me?'

'I'll tell yuh,' said Shelley Caister, turning from

her rolltop desk and crossing to the whiskey bottle. 'Ain't a saloon-strummer this side of the Washbreak who ain't had his pants holed by them scum.' She had poured herself a measure of whiskey, turned again with a sweep of her dress and sipped carefully at the drink. 'Sure, I'll tell yuh about the O'Mara boys, but yuh ain't goin' to like it. Not one bit yuh ain't.'

It had been at that moment that Sheriff McAndrew had blown a drift of smoke from the shadowed corner and stared long and hard into the saloon owner's beautiful blue eyes.

And if looks could have killed there would surely have been a second death in Grateful that day.

TWO

'Did yuh have to? Did yuh *really* have to do that? Damnit, have yuh the remotest idea of what yuh just done? Yuh've as good as set the tinder under this town and posted a notice tellin' where to find the flares! That's what yuh've done.'

The bed creaked woefully under Sam McAndrew's weight as he flopped to the mattress, threw his hat over the plush satin pillows and gazed, red-faced and unblinking, into Shelley Caister's eyes.

The woman patted the soft waves of her yellow hair, hitched the folds of her long dress to her knees, crossed her legs and stared into the mirror of the dressing-table at the reflected anger creasing the sheriff's brow.

'Somebody was goin' to say it sooner or later,' she said softly. 'Might as well have the truth as a version of it.'

'But the O'Maras,' groaned McAndrew, 'them of all vermin. Hell, Shelley, I know yuh for speakin' yuh mind well enough, but yuh could've toned it down a mite. What yuh told them town-hoggers back there—'

'Was as it is, Sam, and yuh can't say other.' The woman stared defiantly into the mirror. 'Can't, can yuh? Can't deny that Orrin O'Mara and his brothers are dirt. Rape, robbery, murder, straight out killin' for killin's sake; abusin' women like they were so much trash. Wanted through any territory they cross – lower than a snake's belly, Sam, and yuh know it.' She snorted. 'Frank Gallons did the world a favour takin' out Clancy O'Mara like he did. Youngest of the miserable tribe of 'em and fast growin' to be the worst.' She paused. 'Even so—'

'Yeah,' drawled the sheriff, 'even so. . . . Yuh can say that again. You know as well as I do they'll be back. Not t'day, not t'morrow, mebbe not next week, next month, but they'll be back, sure as dead men's markers. And it'll be just that: markers spellin' out dead men, many as yuh care to count. Orrin O'Mara won't be thinkin' no other; brothers Sean and Fergil along of him. Sittin' somewhere out there, musin' on it, latherin' up 'til they're fit to burst. . . .' He sighed and eased his weight to his elbows. 'Gallons might've done the world a favour, but he ain't done nothin' for this town, save condemn it to hellfire. Simple as that.'

'So?' said Shelley, fingering the waves of her hair. 'We're a town, ain't we? We got men, we got guns. We ain't for shyin' from a spot of bother, are we?'

'*Spot of bother* . . . hell, them boys wouldn't know a "spot of bother" if they fell across it! They don't spark "bother" – they set the hounds of fury racin' and gnashin', tearin' folk and flesh apart 'til there ain't nothing left, not a limb, not a stick. Know

what they'll do? They'll round up every scumbag,
low-life sonofabitch drifter and gunslinger they can
lay a hand to 'til they're mebbe twenty strong and
then come ridin' in here—'

'We also got the law, Sam,' said Shelley slowly.
'We got you.'

'Oh, sure,' sighed McAndrew. 'We got me. Well,
ain't that somethin'! A middle-aged lawman who's
seen the best years pass him by, who can't stand
straight to pull his pants on, let alone—'

'Gets 'em off easy enough!' smiled Shelley.

'That's as mebbe,' grunted McAndrew. 'T'ain't a
matter in this reckonin'. Plain fact is—'

'Plain fact is, Sam,' said Shelley, turning from
the mirror, 'we got a situation here not of our
makin' but sure as hell of our settlin', and not, I
agree, with a deal in the barrel if yuh take the
likes of Charlie Catches and Ed Murtrey, Orton
Grey, Walt Pond and Nate Simpler as our best
shots. So, question is: if them O'Mara boys are
plannin' on comin' back, what yuh going to do
about it?'

'I'll tell yuh precisely what I ain't goin' to do. I
ain't goin—'

But the roar of the shot from the saloon bar
below him stifled Sam McAndrew's breath as he
sprang from the bed to his feet, glanced quickly at
the woman, and began to sweat.

He crossed to the door with his fingers already
idling at the butt of his holstered Colt.

A rabble of raised voices, the dull spin of a bottle
across the floor, a glass shattering, a chair scrap-

ing, grunts, croaks, the smell of cordite mingling
on the drift of cigar smoke, sweat and liquor, and
then the grating sound of Frank Gallons's voice
slurring round a string of threats.

'Don't nobody reckon me for gettin' lucky with
that sonofabitch gunslinger. Yuh hear me? Yuh
listenin', every last one of yuh? Anybody says I
didn't take that O'Mara scum clean gets the same
as him there – and I ain't foolin', not one bit. Yuh
got it?'

'He's dead, Frank,' called the barman. 'Yuh shot
Harry Miles, and he weren't armed neither.
Damnit, he weren't meanin' nothin' again yuh,
not the way yuh were hearin' it. Bleedin' like a
poked hog, he is. Hell, I ain't never seen so much
blood.'

'There'll be a whole lot more next mule-head
who says I didn't take O'Mara on the draw,'
drawled Gallons. 'So yuh'd best stand back, all of
yuh. Yuh hear? Stand back!'

'No, Frank, you stand back. Right now, and drop
that piece at yuh feet.'

McAndrew loomed like a long shadow at the
head of the stairs to the bar, his Colt tight and
levelled, his gaze steady as a light on Gallons's
face. 'There'll be no more killin', not this day, not
in my town. Drop it!'

Gallons steadied himself against the banister,
swivelled his red-rimmed eyes to the sheriff,
licked at a trickle of liquor at the corner of his
mouth and slanted his lips to a cynical grin.

'Well, now,' he slurred, fighting a drunken sway
on rubbery legs, 'look yuh here, if it ain't the arm

of the law. Don't get y'self about a deal, do yuh? Weren't showin' too much of y'self front of them O'Mara boys, were yuh? Didn't see yuh facin' up to them, nossir. Leaving it to others, were yuh? That the way of it, Sam? Too much for yuh, were they?'

'That's enough,' snapped McAndrew. 'Yuh ain't doin' y'self no good in that sorta talk. Yuh just killed a fella there, and it don't sound like no self-defence to me, so I'm goin' to have to take yuh in, Frank. Ain't nothin' else for it. Yuh'll stand to a fair trial.'

'Like the hell I will!' croaked Gallons, steadying himself again. 'I ain't for goin' down to no yellow-belly law-spinner. Yuh get y'self back to yuh woman, Sheriff. Hide y'self in her skirts, eh, see if yuh can do a deal better there than yuh can out here!'

Gallons's strength to raise his gun to anything like an aim had already drowned in his liquor haze as McAndrew's Colt spat through a fast, single shot that spun the piece from Gallons's fingers to send it clattering across the bar floor.

There were moments then when stares settled on the sheriff's face as if in a swarming mass, when even the tick of the clock seemed to trudge through the silence, when anything, from anybody, anywhere, might have erupted and turned Shelley's Saloon to a brawling cauldron.

'Let's go, Frank,' murmured McAndrew, moving down the stairs as the gathering began to part in silent passage for the lawman and his prisoner.

Three

'Same old story, same old pattern: fella gets to takin' out a gunman and spends the rest of his days provin' it weren't no lucky draw — 'til somebody faster steps out, or the hangman comes callin'.'

Doc Lesters sighed and shook his head forlornly.

'Just ain't no accountin' for a fool in a frenzy of deception. Yuh goin' to hang this one, Sam, or throw him loose to the waitin' lead? Either way, he's turnin' on worn grease. Won't see the fall. Nossir, that he surely will not.'

Doc turned from the cell bars to gaze through the lantern-lit gloom at the slumped bulk of McAndrew seated behind the cluttered desk, waited a moment, then cleared his throat testily.

'Sam, yuh hearin' me? Yuh goin' to hang Frank Gallons or save y'self the bother?'

'He'll hang,' murmured McAndrew, steepling his fingers at his lips, 'if we still got somewhere to do it.'

'Hey, now,' grinned Doc, crossing to the desk, 'what's that supposed to mean? *If we got some-*

where to do it – what sorta talk is that, f'Crissake? Yuh lettin' this O'Mara business eat at yuh?'

'This *O'Mara business*, as yuh put it, ain't no joke, Doc. In fact, it's about as far from a jokin' matter as yuh can get. I wouldn't care to wager a fly to a heap of dung—'

'Sure, sure,' said Doc, raising his arms to calm him, 'I know what yuh thinkin' and I hear what yuh sayin', but what I ain't seein' or hearin' is the Sam McAndrew *I* know. So where's he skulkin', eh? Where's the Sam McAndrew who settled Rockdale, faced the Peterson bunch, personally took out three of 'em and delivered the rest to trial and the Pen back at Denver? Where's *that* Sam McAndrew?'

'That was ten years back and I was younger, fitter and a darn sight thicker-skulled – and it ain't for you to go mention' them days, Doc. Yuh the only one hereabouts who knows about my past. Let's keep it like that, shall we?'

'Have it your way,' shrugged Doc. 'I ain't for sayin' nothin' about Rockdale and the Petersons to nobody, not a livin' soul. On my honour.' His grey eyes twinkled beneath the bushy white brows. 'Don't stop me none from remindin' yuh who yuh are, though, does it? And before yuh go windin' y'self up in another twister, let me just say straight out, no trimmin' at the edges, the Sam McAndrew of ten years back would've known how to handle the situation yuh got here, sure he would. And *he* would've got to doin' it.'

McAndrew collapsed his steepled fingers,

placed his hands flat on the desk and eased back
in the chair. A soft smile flickered at his lips. 'So
what would he have done – by your reckonin', that
is?'

Doc Lesters took a turn round the office, paused
at the window to glance over the already night-lit
street, grunted softly, and came back to the desk.

'The Sam McAndrew who cleaned up the
streets of Rockdale would be takin' this town by
the scruff of its neck and shakin' it to its goddamn
senses,' he said, stiffening his shoulders as he
fingered the twirled tips of his neat moustache.
'*That*'s what that Sam McAndrew would be doin'.'

He waited a moment. ' 'Course, that fella was
younger and a deal hot-headed. Wore his spurs
between the sheets, didn't he? Never crossed his
mind he might get himself killed doin' it. Nossir.
But yuh see, Sam, it's that sorta livin' that primed
yuh for the time when yuh heels ain't scorchin'
the dust quite so much.'

'All very interestin', Doc,' sighed McAndrew,
slipping his fingers through the clutter, 'but it
ain't—'

'Now, o'course, yuh handled this well enough –
so far,' continued Doc dismissively. 'Yuh spotted
Gallons for what he thinks he's grown to, brought
him in, penned him, and mebbe yuh'll get to
hangin' him at that. Good enough. Heat's off for
the time bein'. But you know well as I do, Sam,
this town's startin' to fester, and it'll get worse.
Likes of Murtrey, Catches, Walt Pond, Simpler . . .
hell, they're likely as not gettin' suspicious of
their own shadows right now! Seein' an O'Mara at

every turn, round every corner, and mebbe not so
fussed with you neither.' Doc paused again, his
eyes darkening. 'Yuh've taken out their hero, Sam.
Put the man who shot Clancy O'Mara behind
bars. Now that—'

Doc swung round as the door to the office
crashed open and a sweat-streaked, dishevelled
Gus Coles staggered to the edge of the lantern
glow.

'Need yuh, Sam. Real fast,' he gasped, spinning
sweat from his cheeks. 'Far end of town. We got
trouble. Close to a killin' as a whisker.'

'Keep an eye on things here, Doc,' snapped
McAndrew, coming to his feet. 'Night's still young!'

'Sure,' murmured Doc to himself minutes later
as he watched the sheriff and Coles disappear
into the street shadows, 'night's young enough.
Let's just hope it ain't passed yuh by. . . .'

They were maybe thirty strong, men of the town
and surrounding homesteads; men of all sizes,
shapes and callings; rowdy men, arguing among
themselves, stirring minds and opinions to a
lather, some swigging thoughtlessly from bottles,
some already toting rifles, staves; pushing and
shoving; turning in useless circles; then, as if as
one at a given signal, to the porch of Walt Pond's
rooming-house where, his stubby legs astride a
wooden crate for extra height, Charlie Catches
was calling for quiet.

'Now listen up there, men, listen up,' he called,
waving his arms. 'Hold it, fellas, will yuh? Quiet,
damn yuh!'

The shouting subsided, the movement ceased and the mob fell to silent concentration.

'We got things to talk through,' Catches began again, 'matters to be decided, and we ain't goin' to make no progress if we don't have some sorta order.'

'Get to it, Charlie!' came a shout.

'I am, I am!' snapped the banker, tugging at his waistcoat. 'Fact is—'

'Fact is, Frank Gallons shot an O'Mara and jail ain't no place for him,' came another shout amid yells of agreement. 'No way is it.'

'That's so,' blustered Catches, mopping at a surge of sticky sweat across his face. 'Can't deny it. Most of us seen it, the heck we did. But it's also a fact that Harry Miles—'

'Harry were shootin' his mouth off,' growled a man from the back of the mob. 'He asked for it.'

'Well, mebbe he did at that,' said Catches, 'but more to the point—'

Walt Pond stepped forward to stand at the banker's side. 'We got our town here to protect,' he shouted, raising his arms. 'Our homes, our womenfolk, the young 'uns. We gotta be ready for them O'Mara boys, 'cus they're comin' back, sure enough. Oh, yes, they're comin' back, and we're goin' to finish the job when they do! That right? That so? That what we goin' to do?'

Wild cheering rose on the night. Somebody smashed a bottle. Somebody cracked a bull-whip. A flaming torch streaked through the darkness to fall like a shooting star in the dirt.

A girl screamed.

A child bawled.

A hound moaned.

'Right,' yelled Pond again, 'so how we goin' to do it?

'Now hold on there,' began Catches. 'We gotta think this through. We gotta—'

'First thing we gotta do is get Frank Gallons outa jail,' shouted a barrel-chested hulk of a dust-smeared man stepping to Pond's side. 'That's what we gotta do, and no messin'. We – us, you and me – we gotta be the law round here. Ain't nothin' to be had in trustin' to that mealy-mouthed sheriff no more. He's washed-up. We all seen that. So what we waitin' for?'

More cheering. More yells. The whip cracked again. The girl screamed and then began to giggle.

Charlie Catches lost his balance and toppled from the crate.

Walt Pond turned, disappeared indoors and emerged seconds later with an armful of Winchesters.

'Help y'selves, boys!' he yelled.

Undertaker Orton Grey scurried away to the shadows, his lips murmuring through an incantation nobody heard.

Ed Murtrey ran to his store and double-checked that the doors were locked.

Nate Simpler smoothed a hand over the soft cleft at his chin.

The dust-smeared man grabbed the bull-whip from his partner and dashed away to the head of the mob.

A dozen torches flared over the night and slowly, like the scuffing of a hundred hoofs through the dirt of some underground cavern, the mob moved away, down the street, towards the brighter lights of Shelley's Saloon and the lantern glow at the sheriff's office.

Only then, when the sweat-soaked menace of the men of Grateful was gleaming in the flare and dance of flaming torches, did Sam McAndrew step from the deeper shadows of the boardwalk, cross to the centre of the street, turn and face the mob head on.

His Colt was still holstered.

Four

The mob halted, the torch flames licked the night. Nobody moved, nobody spoke. Only pairs of eyes, some wide and round, some narrowed to slits, stared and glared at the lone figure of Sam McAndrew.

'Goin' some place?' he grunted. 'Somethin' special in mind? Takes a whole heap of yuh, don't it?'

'Yuh can make this easy on y'self, Sam,' said Walt Pond, stepping forward, his Winchester tight in his grip. 'Don't want no blood spilled.'

'Too darned right,' clipped McAndrew. 'So yuh can all go home, can't yuh? Get y'selves some sleep.'

'No, Sam, we ain't for sleepin',' said Murtrey, joining Walt Pond. 'Not yet we ain't. We're for settlin' an issue right now, this night, before another day gets to dawnin'.' He ran his tongue nervously over his lips. 'Best let us get to it.'

'First I heard of it, Ed,' said the sheriff, easing his weight to one leg. 'And just what's so urgent about this issue it takes most of the town to get to it at this hour?'

'It's like this, Sam . . .' flustered Charlie Catches before being shoved aside by Nate Simpler.

'It's the fella yuh holdin' back there,' drawled the man with the bull-whip. 'Frank Gallons. We want him out, yuh hear? Out. Right now. Yuh ain't got no cause—'

'Shootin' an unarmed man is cause enough,' snapped McAndrew. 'Gallons'll stand his trial front of Judge Carver come the next circuit. Meantime, he stays where he is. That's the law – and *I'm* the law, 'case you've forgotten.'

The man flicked the tip of the whip through the dirt. 'Not for much longer yuh ain't,' he croaked, watching the curl of the leather before lifting his gaze in a cold, long stare. 'Yuh all through in this town, McAndrew. Finished. We've had enough.'

'What he means . . .' began Catches.

'Yuh should've done for them O'Mara scum, Sam,' said Pond. 'Should've had the four of 'em for the worms. 'Stead of that—'

' 'Stead of that we got the threat of 'em sittin' in our guts like bad meat,' snapped Murtrey. 'Only Gallons had the nerve to hold firm, and we ain't goin' to stand by watchin' him rot!' The mob murmured and shifted menacingly. 'He ain't going to hang, Sam. May as well face it. So yuh either go unlock that cell door now, or we'll do it for yuh. Suit y'self. Time's runnin' out.'

Charlie Catches shook himself free of the grip of a lean, scar-faced man and stumbled across the dirt. 'Now why don't we just cool this and get to considerin' a more amenable approach? We're all grown men, aren't we? All fellas of the town. Heavens above, we all got our homes here, our lives. It surely ain't in nobody's interest for us to go gettin'—'

The bull-whip cracked across the banker's back throwing him to the ground. McAndrew stepped aside, his hand already at the butt of his Colt, but the roar of Walt Pond's Winchester tossed him back with the ease of a plains' wind chasing loose sage.

The Colt flew uselessly from the sheriff's grip as blood began to spread thick and fast at his shoulder. He grovelled for a moment, slid to his stomach, squirmed, groaned and was lost in the mob's surge forward.

McAndrew was no more than lifeless limbs in the heaving tramp of boots that passed over him then in the rush for the lantern-lit jail.

Doc Lesters rolled his hands thoughtfully through the towel, grunted quietly to himself, glanced carefully at Shelley Caister and then at the silent, sleeping body between the sheets on her bed.

'Goin' to take time,' he said, laying aside the towel. 'Bad wound there. Another half-inch and we'd have been callin' for Orton Grey. Damn it!' He sighed. 'He'll sleep now, but when he wakes. . . . Oh, my, that ain't goin' to be no moment to relish!'

'I'll handle it,' said the woman coming to the side of the bed. 'I've known Sam McAndrew for long enough to get him to listenin' before he gets to doin'. And in this state, he'll listen.'

Doc sighed again, moved to the window over-looking the dark street and peered into the night. 'All quiet now,' he murmured. 'Hell, they gotta be outa their minds to do what they done. Don't make no sense. Only one way for it to go from here on.' He turned to Shelley. 'Yuh'd be wise to think about leavin' town, yuh know that, don't yuh? Get y'self and yuh girls—'

'I ain't goin' no place, Doc. This is my home, my business. Ain't no two-bit scumbags houndin' me outa town. No way.' The woman stiffened and settled her hands on her hips. 'Might have to do somethin' about Sam here, though. Town ain't no place for him to be, not 'til he's recovered. Minute them sonsofbitches get to the cold light of day and realize just where their crazed thinkin's got them, Sam's goin' to be a threat, specially to Frank Gallons.'

'Hmm, see yuh point,' grunted Doc. 'Get him away some place, yuh mean? Coupla weeks'd do the trick with a wound like that. Yuh got a place in mind?'

'Got a cabin out on the Long Sands drift, side of the river. Somewhere to get away from booze, cigars and sweat-soaked men. Not a deal to it, but it's quiet, hidden and the air's fresh.'

'Sounds fine,' said the Doc. 'Don't solve nothin' in the long run, but at least Sam'll have the chance to get his head screwed on again and that shoulder healed.' His gaze settled on the woman's face. 'That's his shootin' arm they've put out, yuh know. Won't be drawin' no Colt in a while.'

'All the more reason to get him clear. First light,

I'd reckon, before the town sobers up.' Shelley
fingered the sheet folds nervously. 'Ain't no tellin'
how this fella's goin' to be feelin' when he gets his
eyes open.'

Doc Lesters reached for his jacket, slipped it on
and closed his medicine bag with a defiant snap.
'I got a pretty good idea,' he grunted. 'And there
are some boots goin' to be walkin' his way I just
wouldn't want to be in.'

'So it's done and that's the sum of it. Ain't no goin'
back. Town's ours.' Walt Pond gazed over the faces
watching him through the gloom of his rooming-
house parlour, sniffed loudly, wiped the sweat
from his cheeks and helped himself to another
measure of whiskey. 'And I ain't regrettin' nothin'.
Not a thing,' he added.

'What about McAndrew,' said Ed Murtrey softly
from somewhere in a deep shadow. 'He ain't goin'
to be pleased none – *if* he's alive.'

' 'Course he's alive,' grunted Charlie Catches,
brushing dirt from his waistcoat. 'I seen Doc
Lesters and Shelley Caister dragging him away.
He weren't dead then, not by a long shot. And
when he pulls through. . . . Well, now, ain't that
goin' to be—'

'Shut yuh whinin', Charlie,' snapped Nate
Simpler, lounging on the door jamb. 'One man
don't make a town, yuh know. Never has. Sam
McAndrew's good days were over long back. We all
seen that. He'd been even half a sheriff he would-
n't never have given them O'Mara boys breathin'

space. He'd have got to 'em long before Frank
Gallons.'

'Yeah, and there's another thing—' began
Catches again.

'We give the badge to Frank,' said Pond flatly.
'That don't need no debatin'.'

'Legally speakin', o'course,' muttered Orton
Grey, adjusting his spectacles, 'accordin', that is to
county law, I ain't certain—'

'Yuh don't have to be,' croaked Murtrey. 'Town's
ours, Orton. We run it fittin' to needs. County law
don't figure. Soon as Frank's sobered up, he gets
the badge, then we start plannin' how to settle
with the O'Maras. Town's with us to a man on
that.'

'Sure they are,' said Catches, 'but there ain't
none of yuh takin' into account on how
McAndrew's goin' to react. Yuh surely don't think
he's just goin' to lie there sleepin' out the day in
them silky sheets of Shelley's, do yuh? Sam
McAndrew might have seen better days, but he
ain't for throwin' out his boots yet awhile.'

'So mebbe we should make damn certain he
ain't no trouble,' grunted Pond.

'What yuh sayin' there?' blinked Charlie. 'If yuh
sayin'—'

' 'Course he is,' grinned Simpler. 'If McAndrew
ain't already dead, I'll wager he ain't no more
than a spit from it. If we gotta hurry it along a
mite, kinda point the fella in the right direction
. . . well, now, who's to stop us?'

'But that'd be outright murder. Ain't no other
word for it.'

'Won't be nothin' alongside of what the O'Mara boys'll be doin' next time they're in town!' scowled Murtrey. 'How'd yuh fancy bein' fried alive, Charlie, or mebbe strung up like a chicken, or gut shot? Mebbe yuh should have a word with Orton here. Get y'self measured for yuh pine while yuh got the chance!'

'We might all be doin' that,' came a voice through the softly breaking first light across the porch. 'Sam McAndrew's just left town, straight as a stave back of a wagon, Shelley along of him. But alive, gentlemen, very much so. Just thought yuh'd like to know.'

The others said nothing as they watched Gus Coles pass on down the empty street where the morning seemed to be coming up a touch greyer than usual.

Five

Doc Lesters watched the first spots of late afternoon rain spread across the dirt like black freckles, stepped into the cover of his back-door porch and narrowed his gaze again on the far horizon.

Getting murky out there now, he thought, almost too grey to fathom shapes let alone movement. No chance of picking out a rider, not until he was close. Might be too late then. Fast rider could be into town before old eyes had spotted him. Even so, might be worth hanging on here till nightfall. You never knew. . . .

He sighed and relaxed against a porch post.

Been nearly a full week now since the shooting of Clancy O'Mara and the night of the mob taking over. Six whole days of Frank Gallons strutting the town behind the sheriff's badge with the civic elders walking in his wake like shadows. Six whole days too with Sam McAndrew holed-up in the Long Sands cabin, Shelley Caister getting to him when she could and reporting back to Doc on his progress.

But progress there was.

'He's eatin', sleepin', movin' about – and startin'

to growl! He's gotta be improvin'!' she had smiled after her last visit. 'Another week and I'll be gettin' to holdin' him down!'

Could be she would at that, thought Doc, but maybe that was not the sort of progress best for anybody's health, certainly not Sam's.

Just what would be festering in that mind of his: a hell-bent determination to claim back his badge and settle with Frank Gallons; put the town elders behind bars, shake the rest of the men of Grateful into sense, and then wait on the O'Mara mob riding out of some godforsaken dusk intent on a bloodbath?

All that with a shooting arm that would take weeks to mend good as new? And just what did Sam McAndrew figure the town elders had been doing and planning meantime?

Not sitting back in gloating satisfaction that was for sure. Leastways, not in Charlie Catches' case. . . .

'Hell, Doc, we got one almighty situation brewin' here,' he had croaked on the night he had sneaked into Doc's back parlour, snatched at gasping breath and wiped the lathering sweat from his brow. 'I'm tellin' yuh, this whole business is outa hand. Right outa hand. There's men struttin' the street who ain't got a pinch of sense no more. Addled with power and not content to rest 'til they got more. Hell. . . . Frank Gallons ain't no lawman, won't never be neither, but there ain't a mouth hereabouts who'd say other. And I'll tell yuh straight up, he intends holdin' on to that badge to the death.

'Don't know where Sam McAndrew's hiding out
– and don't want to neither,' Catches had sweated
on, 'but if he so much as sets a foot in this town,
gets even to spittin' distance of it, he's a dead
man, Doc. And that is plain fact. Tell yuh somethin' else, somebody's gotta do somethin' about it.
Got to.'

He had paused, mopped at more sweat and
waved a loose, empty hand. 'I don't know. . . . Just
somethin'. . . . Somethin' that gets us back to
sense. Mebbe get somebody here. Send for somebody. Fella with a firm, steady grip. Or mebbe
somebody who'd put the fear of Hell into men's
cacklin' brains. And do it fast. . . .'

Question was, pondered Doc, squinting against
the rain, had Charlie Catches done just that?

He eased himself clear of the porch post and
raised a hand to shield his eyes in one last scan of
the horizon, fast disappearing now in the grey
murk of nightfall and bad weather. Another half-
hour and it would be gone. Nobody with any sense
would be out there of his choosing through the
sort of night coming up, not unless he had ridden
far and had only Grateful to reach. And not,
thought Doc through a grunt, unless he was
coming of somebody's calling, with a mission in
mind.

But maybe Charlie had not been that commit-
ted to his thinking. On the other hand, he was a
banker, and a smart one at that, and sometimes
found it useful to not always let the right hand
know what the left hand was doing.

Just so long as he did.

'Yuh here for business, mister, or just socializin',
'cus if it's the former you're way out of pasture,
and if it's all social you're 'bout as welcome as a
dung bug!'

Shelley Caister folded her arms dramatically
across her tight cleavage, leaned back on the
closed door of her bedroom above the saloon bar
and stared like a mean she-cat at Frank Gallons.

'Either way,' she added, 'I'm throwin' yuh out.
So shift yuh fat butt off them clean sheets there
and walk!'

'Tough talk, ma'am,' grinned Gallons leaning
back on one elbow, 'but t'ain't of a deal of 'count,
not from where I'm sittin'.' He ran his fingers idly
over the sheets. 'However, since yuh askin', let's
say I just stepped outa that rain-licked night out
there and figured I'd exercise my sheriff's rights,
so to speak.' His dark gaze settled slowly on
Shelley's face. 'Yuh were Sam McAndrew's
woman, weren't yuh? This *was* his place, weren't
it?' He patted the bed. 'And seein' as how I'm
wearin' the badge now—'

'F'get it, Gallons,' snapped Shelley. 'Yuh ain't fit
to stand in Sam's shadow, let alone reckon on
walkin' with it, so just get out. Right now!'

Gallons shrugged loosely and traced a grubby
finger over the sheets. 'Suit y'self, ma'am, I ain't in
no hurry. You and me got all the time we're goin'
to need. Long days and even longer nights. . . .'
The finger halted and stiffened. 'But what I ain't
got the time to dally over is the matter of where

yuh got McAndrew holed-up.' The dark gaze lifted again. 'You do have him holed-up, don't yuh, ma'am? I mean, I ain't imaginin' that, am I?'

'Go to hell!' sneered the woman.

'Oh, sure,' smiled Gallons. 'I guess we'll all be doin' that when the reckonin' comes, but meantime—'

'Sam McAndrew's alive and well enough and he'll be back, you bet on it!' said Shelley, and regretted the outburst instantly as she unfolded her arms and pushed herself away from the door.

'Well, now, is that a fact?' drawled Gallons. 'Alive, eh? My, my, that could be troublesome. Oh, yes, real troublesome. And just where might the fella be makin' this remarkable recovery? Not in town. Not hereabouts. So where? Yuh happen to have a notion, ma'am?'

'I wouldn't—' began Shelley, her cheeks flushed and damp with a clinging sweat.

'Oh, but you would, ma'am, and you will.' Gallons came slowly to his feet. ' 'Cus the alternative don't bear thinkin' about.'

'Do yuh worst, yuh won't get—'

'Now, the way I figure it,' said Gallons, moving to the door and standing with his back to it, 'I could get real rough with you, ma'am. And I mean rough, so's yuh'd be takin' to that temptin' bed there kinda permanent. But that would be an awful waste. So what say we torch this whole place to ash, eh? Every last stick of it, and just happen to overlook them pretty gals of yours who somehow got themselves trapped in here? T'ain't a comfortin' thought now, is it, ma'am?'

'You sonofabitch!' spat Shelley.

'Shall we talk?' grinned Gallons.

There was still a spit of that night's rain on the chill air an hour before sun-up when Walt Pond mounted his newly purchased roan mare and reined her nose west from the back of the rooming-house to the trail for the Long Sands drift.

He was glad of the cool, misty rain on his face. It eased the hot sweating that had been there since the meeting with Gallons and the others in Murtrey's store. Eased too the raging thoughts pounding his head on just how, when it came to it, he would go about finishing Sam McAndrew. Pity of it was that his shot in the street had not done the job right there and then. Now he would have the thankless task of shooting an already wounded man.

Not, of course, as he had told the others when Gallons had brought the news of where the one-time sheriff was holed-up, that he was flinching from the job. No, it had to be done, for all their sakes, sooner the better, and he was the one to do it. Only fitting. When a town turned on its lawman, there could be no looking back.

Consolation was, he guessed, that no harm had come to Shelley Caister and her girls. She had talked readily enough under Gallons's 'persuasion' and was still in one desirable piece. Hell, who could say, time might come once this was all over, when the woman would get to casting an eye for the prospect of settling down. She would be some catch for the quieter days.

Quieter days, he mused. . . . Well, they might be sometime on yet. There was McAndrew to deal with, the O'Mara bunch to handle, town to lick into shape, a whole new way of going on to be fashioned.

And Charlie Catches.

Sure, he pondered, there was Charlie. He was beginning to behave real strange, like he was ranging his thoughts round other things, in other places. Never could bottom Charlie. He was all debit and credit, with the emphasis on the credit – to his account!

Somebody should keep an eye out for Charlie Catches. Meantime, there was this day, the cool rain and the cabin at Long Sands.

Sam McAndrew would be dead before noon.

Six

The fire in the forge at Gus Coles's livery had needed attention early that morning. Town might be going stark raving mad, Gus had thought, but that was no good reason for the day-to-day business of it to suffer. Somebody would be needing something of him sooner or later. Life and the means of getting through it went on in spite of the likes of Frank Gallons and the civic elders, and no amount of sweating over the threat of the O'Mara boys, real or imagined, was going to change things. Horses would still need looking to, tools repaired, the everyday bits and pieces made good again.

Damn it, he had reflected, fellow could get to sitting long enough in the shadows to become one!

And so it was that Gus was tending the forge almost before the first touch of light was creeping out of the east. Rain was still a spit on the keen morning air, but he figured for a dry, hot day coming up, the sort of day he would have relished under normal circumstances. But 'normal' had seemed to have taken to its sick bed of late. Just no telling what this day might turn up. You had to take it as it came and be thankful for the chance.

He had turned a half-hour or so later from the already glowing bed of fresh embers to begin the drudge of mucking out, when the soft, steady thud of approaching hoofbeats had brought him the few steps to the side of the building and a clear view over the sweep of land beyond.

Hardly a thing to be seen at first glance; same spread of empty dirt, scattered rocks, untidy brush, a nowhere place spilling out to nowhere in particular. No trail worth the taking going out, none a fellow would follow coming in.

But somebody was on it that morning.

And maybe more than one, Gus had reckoned, as he watched and waited, eyes narrowed, grip tight on the rake in his right hand, hearing concentrated on the beat hidden in the half light.

It was a full five minutes before Gus had a shape to focus on. Riders, sure enough; two fellows coming at a measured, unhurried pace, heading clean as a whistle for town.

Well, now, he pondered, and just who might be figuring on Grateful for a haven, or a refuge, come to that, at this hour? Not the O'Maras; not just two of them; not this easy. Not Sam McAndrew. Not nobody, when you reckoned it through, of this town, or even this territory. No, these riders were strangers, newcomers from some place else.

The law, he wondered? Supposing some marshal had got to hear of the fate of Sheriff McAndrew. Supposing he was riding in right now to settle things, get that badge off Frank Gallons's shirt, take them shallow-gutted civic leaders down a peg or two and straighten them out. Well, and not before time, not if this town was going to stay in one piece. . . .

Not the law, Gus decided minutes later. Nothing like the law judging by the look of these fellows as they came into sharper focus. Tall men; dirt and stubble-shaded faces; rough dress, and ironed to the hilt with Colts and rifles. Might be drifters, out-of-luck gamblers, gunslingers even, but still in no hurry. Nobody hounding their butts, leastways not close.

So just who?

Gus stood his ground as the riders approached, slowing to a canter at the sight of him, then to a reined-back walk and a final halt once within hailing distance.

'Come far?' asked Gus through a ready smile. 'Don't get many headin' from this quarter. Strangers hereabouts?'

The men sat their mounts without moving, silent and watchful as if taking the blacksmith apart.

'Mite early for the saloon,' Gus added holding the smile. 'But Walt Pond's roomin'-house gets to breakfastin' first light. Coffee'll be simmerin' right now. Say, come to mention it, so's mine, back there on the forge. You fellas for takin' a mug? Guess yuh would be, eh? Ridden through the night? Sure as hell rained some. We ain't had rain like that—'

'Charlie Catches hereabouts?' drawled the swarthier, heftier man.

'Charlie?' frowned Gus. 'The banker? Sure, Charlie Catches lives here. Most likely snorin' on, knowin' him! Ain't one for stirrin' 'til the sun's warmed his money. That's Charlie! But, sure, yuh'll find his place side of Murtrey's store. He a friend of yours?'

'Yuh might say that,' drawled the man again, aiming a fount of spittle to the dirt.

'Charlie's a popular fella round town, him bein' the bank man and that,' smiled Gus. 'Fella yuh tend to need more than the doc, eh? Yeah. . . . 'Course we had some bother here lately. Not that yuh would've heard, I guess, comin' a distance. All started—'

'McAndrew – he in town?' asked the second man, fingering a nervous twitch in his cheek.

Gus swallowed carefully. 'Sheriff McAndrew ain't exactly about right now. He kinda, well, I guess yuh'd say he had an accident, sorta. Nothin' time won't put to rights.' Gus swallowed again. 'Yuh know how it gets. . . .' He paused. 'You fellas ain't the law by any chance, are yuh? 'Cus if yuh are—'

The swarthy man spat again. 'Side of Murtrey's store, yuh say?' he croaked.

'Oh, Charlie? Sure, side of the store,' blustered Gus, turning to face the street. 'Yuh want me to go—'

'We'll find our own way,' said the man, urging his mount to a walk.

'Can't miss it,' murmured Gus watching the men go. 'Right there, on yuh left. But like I say, Charlie ain't one for stirrin'. . . .' He wiped a sudden beading of sweat from his top lip. 'What the hell,' he muttered to himself, 'Yuh come this far, what's a few more yards? Who cares, anyhow?'

He did, and he knew it.

Doc Lesters paced anxiously to the far end of his front parlour, sighed through his long stare at the space of blank wall, grunted and turned sharply to face Shelley Caister.

'Ain't happy 'bout lettin' yuh do this, yuh know,' he said, clasping his hands behind him. 'T'ain't no job for a woman, specially a good-lookin' woman. If I were twenty years younger—'

'If you were twenty years younger, Doc,' smiled Shelley, 'yuh'd be darn fool enough to go askin' me to wed yuh and I'd be fool enough to say "Yes" and stand here watchin' my man saddle up for the job I'm goin' to do 'cus you're too old. Got it? Now, check over that Colt there while I slide m'self into these ridin' pants. And no lookin' neither!'

'But, Shelley—' began Doc again.

'But nothin'. Just do as I say. We lost too much time as it is.'

'You're a good three hours, mebbe more, behind Pond. If he—'

'I know where I am and where I'm goin' and what I got to do,' said Shelley, struggling into the pants as Doc turned to check and load the Colt. 'I also know that sendin' out Walt Pond to settle with Sam is Frank Gallons's first big mistake. Walt ain't going to summon the guts for a cold-blooded killin' that easy. It'll take him a whole heap of time. Good, 'cus I can use all he'll waste.'

She released a deep breath. 'There. How'd I look?'

'Goddamnit, woman, this ain't no occasion for wonderin' how yuh *look*,' sighed Doc.

'Woman don't go no place if she don't look right – golden rule of winnin'. I know!' She paused a moment and closed her eyes. 'Should've made sure I did a bit more winnin' against that sono-fabitch Gallons, 'stead of. . . . Damn it! What's done's done.' She opened her eyes again. 'Thanks for yuh help, Doc. Couldn't have got m'self ready like this front of all them probin' eyes at the saloon. You keep a watch on things here, will yuh? Just let me get to Sam, help him, get that Colt there into line against Pond and—'

'Hold it,' snapped Doc crossing hurriedly to the parlour window and peering through it. 'Hell!' he murmured.

'Trouble?' asked Shelley.

'You bet on it,' croaked Doc. He stepped aside and stared fearfully into the woman's eyes. 'Get y'self out the back, onto that horse of yours and ride like yuh ain't never done before. And when yuh get to Sam, and if he's still alive, tell him Wino Keets and Casey Brett have hit town. He'll know what yuh mean and what to do – and, God willin', live long enough to do it!'

Seven

The lick of misty rain across Walt Pond's face had long been replaced by the first sweat of the day as he rode at an easy pace into the cleft of boulders and reined up to rest in the shade.

The roan mare snorted, tossed her head and pawed impatiently at the dirt. She was enjoying this, he thought, slipping from the saddle to stretch his tired limbs. Sure she was; land was open, morning fresh, pace steady. No effort, no stress. He only wished he could say the same for himself. This, as far as he was concerned, was all stress, all effort. No point in not admitting to it.

All very well to think of McAndrew sprawled on his bed down there at the cabin cursing the nag and ache of his wound, wondering how long it might be before he got to handling a Colt again, standing steady enough to aim it, seeing his target sharp and clear. All looked simple enough for the full-bodied fellow who was going to walk up to him and put a bullet clean between his eyes.

Not so easy the longer you got to thinking on it.

What if McAndrew had gained enough strength to stand? What if he had a Colt belted to him?

What if he could *use* it? What if, when it came to
it, the whole thing turned into some lead-spitting
shooting match? What then? Who would be standing come the end of it?

Walt Pond wiped the sweat from his face,
patted the mare's neck and squinted into the first
morning glare. Going to be a dry day, he reckoned.
Clear skies, high sun – and gathering heat. You
could say that again! Real hot come midday, in
more senses than one.

He grunted, mounted up and reined the horse
back to the open land. River lay less than an
hour's ride away. The mare could already smell it
and was keen to be there.

But, then, she was not doing the shooting, was
she?

Charlie Catches was still buttoning his waistcoat
as he hurried through the off-street shadows and
headed for Doc Lesters' back door.

Hell, he was thinking, he had pulled off some
deal and no mistake. Imagine it, two hard-living,
hard-hitting, no-messing gunmen right here in
Grateful. Men of the world, professional to the
butts of their polished Colts. Men who knew how
to handle men, no matter what their kind, who
stood for no nonsense where order was concerned;
who could even *stare* a fellow into submission.

Men who had seen it all before, ugly as it ever
got, been there, done it, settled it. Protection –
that was it, a shield of firm resolve and, should it
be needed, scorching lead against the likes of
anybody who stepped tall-headed and arrogant

from the boardwalk. Yessir, men who would boot the O'Maras – and others along of them should they be so inclined – clean out of the territory.

That was the way to do things round here. Get to it, make decisions, stir the action!

Sure, the fellows came expensive, but nothing worth the having came cheap. Hell, close on thirty years in banking had taught him that. No, if you selected from the top, you paid top price. And he would. Oh, yes, Charlie Catches would pay for the salvation of Grateful out of his own pocket if need be. Well, near as damn it.

Some deal! Just wait till Doc heard! Wino Keets and Casey Brett at the town's beck and call, and no questions asked. Now if that was not the smartest, neatest slice of dealing he had ever had the good fortune, and the brains, to put his hand to, then he for one would—

'*Yuh brainless idiot!*' Doc Lesters' croaked curse hissed from the porch shadows like a rattler with a liver turmoil.

'Get in here, will yuh, and close the door real quiet behind yuh!'

The smile on Charlie Catches' face had faded behind a brimming sweat long before his eyes had adjusted to the parlour gloom, but not before he had seen the anger firing through Doc Lesters' cheeks.

'I was on my way—' spluttered Charlie.

'Have yuh got the vaguest, slimmest notion of what yuh done?' croaked Doc. 'Yuh got *any* idea at all? No, yuh haven't, not a spit-lick.'

'Now hold on there, Doc—'

'No, you hold on there, Charlie Catches, and I'll
tell you just what yuh done; spell it out, down to
the last dung-dark drop of dirt.'

'Yuh ain't got no way of figurin', and this ain't
none of yuh—'

'Business?' hissed Doc. 'None of my business,
Charlie? That what yuh sayin'? Well, I'll tell yuh,
this is *my* business, right through. All the way.
And I'll tell yuh why: 'cus them mud-bellied
sonsofbitches yuh brought into town – Wino Keets
and Casey Brett – are here for just one reason,
and one only. Know what that is, Charlie? To kill
Sam McAndrew.'

Charlie Catches' brimming sweat lathered to a
flood that sparkled like ice on his brow. His mouth
opened, but he made no audible sound.

'So yuh went ahead and did it, didn't yuh,
Charlie?' said Doc, pacing slowly round the sweating banker. 'Went ahead and, like yuh told me, did
somethin'; sent for somebody "who'd put the fear
of Hell into men's cacklin' brains". And yuh sure
as the Devil's teeth did that!

'How'd yuh do it, Charlie? Wire one of yuh
bankin' contacts over at Denver? Send one of yuh
clerks from here? Don't matter none. It's what
yuh got, what yuh payin' for that counts. And
believe me, fella, the price is goin' to be awful
high. Just about as high as it gets.'

'Yuh got this all wrong, Doc,' groaned Charlie.
'We need them sorta fellas right now. Town needs
'em.'

'Like it does the plague!' flared Doc. 'Them
fellas – scum more like – couldn't give a damn for

this town or any other. They're here to kill McAndrew, to set right a sore that's been festerin' for ten years.' He halted and stared into Charlie's face. 'They're here for a reckonin', Charlie, and it's goin' to make the O'Mara boys' rampage look like a quiet supper in some preacher's back parlour!'

'That's talk, Doc, all talk. Why, them fellas ain't—'

'Rockdale,' snapped Doc. 'The Peterson gang. Yuh recollect, Charlie? No? Too busy bankin', were yuh? Pity. Yuh could've saved us a whole heap of hell-fire. It was there, in Rockdale, that Sheriff Sam McAndrew settled an issue that finished the gang for good. Three dead, eight jailed in the Pen at Denver – among them Wino Keets and Casey Brett who vowed, as they went down, to get even with Sam minute they stepped free.'

Doc paused and swallowed deeply. 'Bet them fellas couldn't believe their luck when a banker offered to pay 'em to come here, straight to Sam McAndrew's front door! Well done, Charlie, well done – damn yuh!'

Charlie Catches ran a shaking hand over the lathering sweat. 'But I wasn't to know that, was I, f'Crissake? Hell, all I was doin'—'

There was a sudden, spitting volley of gunfire from somewhere in the street. A yell, a shout, crazed laughter and a woman's scream.

'And yuh've done it, ain't yuh, Charlie?' murmured Doc. 'Hear that? We're just gettin' started. . . .'

Eight

Walt Pond's reflection of his face in the still rock-pool a few yards short of the swirling river was not a pretty sight. Even he had to admit it. Damn it, if he had not known better he would have sworn the face there on the glassy surface was somebody else. Some fella who looked as if he had seen a ghost – the grey death mask of himself.

Hell, and now he was shaking!

He eased back from the pool to the shade below a shelving of rock, snuggled into it and turned a slow, anxious gaze upriver to the lonely bulk of the log cabin. No sign of life there, he mused. No curl of smoke from the chimney, doors and windows shut tight, no movements, no sounds. Place might have been deserted.

Leastways, Sam McAndrew would like anybody coming close to think so.

A trembling half-smile flitted across his lips. Well, he for one was not fooled. McAndrew was in there, sure enough. Fellow in his state, with a wound like a stone slab sitting on his shoulder,

was going no place. About as far as that shaded
veranda, he thought; just the few steps to take in
the fresh air, watch the sun come up, see it go
down. Maybe smoke a cigar, roll his tongue round
some whiskey, ponder on just how long he was
going to be holed up here.

Get used to the idea of forever, thought Walt,
through another half-smile.

He shifted, wondered if the mare was still safe
hitched back there in the rocks, ran his fingers
over the butt of his holstered Colt and came carefully from the shade to the glare.

Then waited.

Temptation was to get this over with fast and
high-tail it at a pace for town. Gallons would be
getting anxious, Ed Murtrey pacing his store,
Nate Simpler honing that razor till it was damn
near ready to snap, Orton Grey murmuring sense-
lessly, and Charlie Catches up to no good for
certain.

Another sound reason to be in town was
Shelley Caister. Somebody had to look to her
before Gallons got notions above his station, or
them O'Mara boys rode in and took a shine to her.

Still, there was no real need to rush, was there?
Day was still new and, hell, just how long did it
take to shoot a fellow? Over in seconds once that
trigger finger took the pressure. . . . One shot,
turn, and walk away. Anybody could do it.

He just wished he could stop shaking. Must be
the heat.

Walt had taken no more than a dozen steps
towards the cabin when he paused again, this

time narrowing his gaze on what had seemed to be a movement back of the place.

Hardly likely, he reckoned, not unless some animal was scavenging there, or maybe a bird strutting out for lunch. Place was remote enough for almost anything wild to be on the move, save, of course, anything wild *and* human. No, if there had been a movement it was certain to be doing it on four legs.

He eased on, still shaking, still sweating.

He would not draw the Colt till the last, he thought. No point. Hell, what did he expect McAndrew to do: bound from his cot like a kid and launch himself at the intruder? Some chance!

In this heat, at this hour, fellow was probably sleeping; muttering through some dream there of Shelley Caister. Sure, that would be McAndrew, still clinging to the fond hope that all would get back to normal just given time. All he had to do was rest and sleep and dream on. . . .

Sweet dreams, mister!

It took Walt another three minutes to reach the shaded veranda and only seconds then to pause, wait, listen, and step to the cabin door.

It swung open to his touch like an invitation.

Hell, it was dark in there. Place smelled too; dusty, musty, faint touch of baccy smoke, cooking, whiskey, sweat. Somebody should get to opening a window. Maybe there was nobody strong enough to reach it.

Walt stepped inside, blinked, squinted, then stared wide-eyed and suddenly bewildered.

The place was deserted, the bed empty.

Somebody had been here, sure enough, and recently, perhaps only an hour or so back. Bed had been slept in; it was still warm! Bloodstained bandaging there on the chair. But where, damn it, was McAndrew?

Walt turned, anxious now, the sweat cold on his face, his fingers fumbling and uncertain as he drew the Colt. The movement, he thought, licking his lips, the one he had seen back of the cabin, must have been McAndrew getting clear. Maybe he had heard something, spotted a shadow. But, hell, if he could move like that, he could just as easily. . . .

Slip of a rock disturbed by a boot. Out there, beyond the veranda, close to the river. McAndrew moving again!

Walt had stumbled back to the veranda and was swinging his gaze to left and right when a fist-size boulder thudded at his feet and rolled across the heat-creaking boards to the door.

'Hell!' he cursed, and blazed two shots high and wild and into nowhere.

Walt stumbled on, into the rocks now, his eyes filling with a new surge of sweat, his legs heavy and dragging at the bulk of his weight.

'No point in prolongin' this, McAndrew,' he called, his voice hollow and cracked. 'Yuh ain't goin' nowhere, I see that. Step out easy and I promise yuh won't feel a thing. It'll be quick, yuh got my word on it.'

Another boulder skimmed through the air and clattered to his feet.

'Don't be a fool. Minute I get yuh fixed, you're a

dead man, yuh know that. So why don't yuh save y'self the pain of waitin'? Can't be no fun out there in this heat, state you're in. Should've made a better job of it first time round, eh? Yuh got my apologies on that, fella. Won't happen again!'

Walt jumped aside as a flatter, sharper stone cleaved through the glare like a blade.

'Goddamnit!' he hissed and released another blazing burst of shots, only to see the lead spit uselessly into the slow flow of the river. 'Can't keep this up, yuh know,' he called. 'Ain't gettin' us nowhere, McAndrew, 'specially y'self. All a waste of time, ain't it? Just stretchin' things out.'

He jumped again, but too late to dodge a stone that cracked across his upper arm. That was it, he groaned inwardly. Enough was enough. Made no sense for a fellow with a Colt to be in some crazy stand-off with a man slinging stones. And, hell, the stone-thrower was wounded at that!

Get to it, Walt Pond, he told himself. Get yourself to that bulge of rocks there, dig out McAndrew like you would a winged animal. Put the miserable soul out of his misery. Nothing to it. All you got to do is get the fellow to raise his head, then one steady, careful shot would do it and this whole mess of a day could be forgotten.

He stepped gingerly across the rocks, arms spread for balance, eyes flitting quickly from a place for safe footholds to the bulge of rocks ahead. Just how had McAndrew managed this so fast, he wondered? How come the fellow had been able to get from the cabin to here without spilling blood? Damn it, you would have thought—

'Far enough, Walt,' came the snap of the voice. 'Hold it right there.'

Walt swayed, steadied himself, peered through the blur of sweat-swimming eyes, blinked and released a curse that hissed from his gut like steam under pressure.

'Shelley Caister!' he gasped, blinking again as the woman eased clear of the rock cover to face him, a Colt tight in her grip at her hip. 'How the hell—?'

'Took the long trail, did yuh?' grinned Shelley. 'Figured yuh might. Said as how yuh'd need time to get to this.'

'Stand clear, Shelley,' croaked Walt. 'This ain't nothin' concernin' you. Just point me to McAndrew.'

'He ain't available right now. Moved him some place a mite safer, so whatever yuh gotta say or do it's me yuh dealin' with.'

'Damnit, Shelley, yuh can't—'

'Oh, but I can, Walt, no problem. And I will.' Shelley took a step forward. 'Now, we goin' to do this in a civilized manner, or is it goin' to get messy? I ain't fussed. Choice is yours.'

Walt swayed again and licked at the sweat. 'High stakes here,' he murmured. 'Yuh know that, don't yuh? Ain't no edge 'tween us, though. We can sort this.'

'No sortin', Walt. Sam McAndrew wants yuh taken in. Yuh'll stand trial along of the rest.'

'Yuh reckon so? Too far gone for that, Shelley. Times change, folk with 'em.' Walts eyes narrowed. 'I ain't never stood to a woman before,' he croaked, 'but I guess—'

Walt Pond's sudden stiffening, the upward flash of his gun hand, tightening of the line of his lips, were probably the fastest movements he had made that day. They came easy, intended, without a second thought as if in that single moment he had spread his whole life on the line.

No going back then. Only the shape of the woman, the Colt in her grip, the look in her eyes and the hot, searing glare of the day. All the rest would be the future.

But it never got started.

Walt saw the blaze of Shelley Caister's gun, heard the roar, felt the soft pressure of his finger on the trigger of his own piece, and knew, even before he was through, that he had been too slow, too late.

Shelley watched the body hit the rocks and waited only long enough then to be certain that Walt Pond, face-down in a rippling rockpool, was as dead as he was ever going to get.

Nine

Gus Coles had it all clear as a bell tolling deep in his head what he had to do. No question, no thinking on. Just resolve it and do it. They could get to reckoning on the wisdom or otherwise of it later. Point was, by then it would be done and the blood of it, if that was what it came to, well worth the spilling. Better that than a living hell.

He grunted, turned up the glow of the lantern and rummaged deeper into the dusty depths of the old shack back of the livery.

It was there all right, wrapped, packed safe and dry as the day he had taken it in, a whole box of the stuff. Dynamite – enough to blow half the town to Kingdom come. He sighed as he ran a hand gently over the lid. Never reckoned on the day dawning when he would have figured on putting a payment-in-kind to such a grisly use. But, he reasoned, when the needs must. . . .

What the hell; it was a way out, one the townsfolk might get to thanking him for when the time came; when it was all they had against sheer terror.

He sighed again as he stared at the lid. He had accepted the box from a wagon family down on their luck in exchange for a new wheel. Some deal! What had the fellow wanted with dynamite aboard his wagon in the first place, unless he was planning on a future in mining somewhere, and just when and where, he had wondered at the time, would a liveryman find a use for it?

Now he knew. Could see it plain as the dust on the lid.

Only way Grateful was going to settle the issue of the O'Mara threat and rid itself in the same blow of the scumbag gunslingers Charlie Catches had brought into town, was to fight back. Anyway, anyhow they could. This might be a way.

And when the smoke had cleared and the dust settled, maybe they would find they had got real lucky and taken out Frank Gallons along of the rest of the dirt. All it needed then was for Sam McAndrew to step into town and take back his badge. . . . Damn it, he was getting ahead of himself! There was this day not yet done and, judging by the noise coming out of the street right now, hotting itself up for a scorching night.

'Hell!' he murmured, as he turned from the box, doused the lantern and left the dusty shack. And you could say that again!

'Yuh wearin' the badge, Frank. Yuh got the edge. So what yuh goin' to do? Shoot 'em or jail 'em?'

Nate Simpler shafted a line of cigar smoke through his clenched teeth and settled a hard gaze on Frank Gallons seated uncomfortably behind the desk in the sheriff's office.

'And Charlie Catches along of 'em while you're at it,' drawled Ed Murtrey. 'And when that's done, yuh can get to findin' out why Walt ain't back from that cabin yet. Seems to me—'

'Just hold it, will yuh,' snapped Gallons, reaching for the half-empty bottle of whiskey and pouring himself a measure. 'We got things to think through.'

'Tonsil varnish ain't goin' to help none,' said Murtrey, crossing the room to the window. 'Unless, o'course, yuh ain't got the stomach for facin' it out.'

'That's enough, Ed,' clipped Simpler. 'Frank's right, we gotta think it through.' He blew another shaft of smoke. Charlie's gotta be out of his mind bringin' in them vermin. Hell, they've good as taken over Shelley's place. And just where is she, f'Crissake?'

'At that cabin,' muttered Murtrey, peering through the window. 'Don't take no workin' out. Yuh should've kept her under lock and key, Frank. Mistake not to. No tellin'—'

'Yuh want this badge, Ed, yuh got it!' flared Gallons. 'Don't reckon for me standin' in yuh way.'

'Don't see yuh standin' to nothin' right now. But time's comin'. Oh, yes, it's comin'.'

'I'm for one of us ridin' out to find Walt,' said Simpler, examining the glowing end of the cigar. 'Meantime, we take in them scum, fast as we can.'

'You volunteerin', Nate?' asked Murtrey. 'Or ridin' out?'

'I'll do whatever—'

Murtrey turned sharply from the window.
'Sure, sure,' he drawled. 'Yuh'll do whatever's
safest for yuh own skin, Nate, same as we all will.'
His gaze shifted darkly. 'Gettin' to be big, ain't it?
Yuh take a bite and before yuh know it, yuh got a
whole mouthful yuh can't chew on. That right?
Sure it is. And we ain't even got to the O'Maras
yet, have we? What happens when they make a
move? We goin' to stand here *thinking it through?*
Doubt if the O'Maras are goin' to wait on that.
So. . . .' He turned back to the window. 'Like I say,
Frank, you got the badge – and seein' on what's
comin' down the street right now, I'd say yuh goin'
to need all the edge yuh can lay a hand to. Drink
up while yuh got the chance.'

'Now steady up there, fellas. Don't let's get hasty,
eh? Mebbe we should consider, have ourselves
another drink. Anythin' yuh fancy.'

Charlie Catches hovered and scuttled like an
uncertain fly round the steps of Wino Keets and
Casey Brett as they made their steady, dirt-scuff-
ing, leather-creaking way down the street towards
the sheriff's office.

'Sure,' spluttered Charlie, stumbling ahead of
the men, stepping clear of their path, wiping the
sweat from his cheeks, 'yuh doin' a good job. I
mean, it's what yuh here for, ain't it? What yuh
gettin' paid for. Yuh know yuh jobs, sure enough,
and ain't nobody sayin' other, but mebbe we
should get to workin' to some sorta plan, eh? Look
through the alternatives. Heck, I sure as hell

know the value of the credit and debit side of things. Why, I been doin' it for—'

The men halted, their dark, hooded stares tight on Charlie's lathered face. 'Yuh complainin', Mr Catches?' mouthed Keets. 'Ain't things to yuh likin?'

'Complainin'?' grinned Charlie. 'Hell, no, I ain't complainin', not one bit. I ain't no cause for that. All I'm sayin' is—'

'Why don't yuh get y'self back to that cosy saloon?' drawled Brett. 'Go warm up some of them gals for when we're all through here. Yuh can leave this to us, Mr Catches. Just tidyin' up.'

'I'm sure I can,' spluttered Charlie again. 'Never doubted it. It's just that. . . .'

The men moved on, their gazes fixed on the door of the office, their hands loose at their sides.

Charlie stumbled ahead, turned through a full circle, began to walk backwards. 'Frank Gallons – now he ain't nothin' alongside the likes of you. Frank . . . why, he ain't nobody, just a fella who got to fancyin' he could wear that badge. Even so, mebbe we should. . . .'

He groaned as the men brushed past him, ran his hands over his cheeks and groaned again as the office door opened and Nate Simpler stepped to the boardwalk.

'Evenin', fellas,' smiled Simpler flourishing his cigar at his lips. 'Lookin' for somebody? Anythin' I can do?'

'You Frank Gallons?' drawled Keets.

'No, name's Simpler, Nate Simpler. Got m'self the barberin' shop back of yuh. Say, if you fellas are lookin' for—'

'If yuh ain't Gallons, we ain't interested,' clipped Brett. 'He in there?'

'Sure he is,' grinned Nate through a cloud of curling smoke. 'But Sheriff Gallons is occupied right now. Town business, yuh know. Gets awful hectic. Still, as a town elder and property man hereabouts, if there's anythin' I can do—'

'There ain't,' spat Keets. 'Best yuh can do, mister, is step aside.'

'Well now, we ain't in the habit . . .' began Nate, and croaked on his words as he watched a Colt come to life in Brett's hand. 'Hey, now there ain't no need—'

'Yuh steppin' aside, mister, or ain't yuh?' snapped Keets. 'One choice. We ain't waitin'.'

Nate Simpler dropped his cigar, glanced wildly round him, opened his mouth as if to speak and crumpled without a sound under the blaze and roar of Brett's gun.

'Gallons, yuh in there?' called Keets, lounging his weight to one leg. 'Don't trip over the body here as yuh step out.'

Ten

He had stayed lucky, but the luck was on a tight rein and fast shortening to nowhere. 'Hell,' croaked Ed Murtrey, settling his shaking hands on the bottle before splashing another measure of whiskey into the glass and lifting it to his lips. 'Yeah,' he groaned through a long swallow, 'It's that sure enough.'

He replaced the glass on the counter of the shuttered, darkened store and peered into the heavy gloom. There was nobody there, nobody even close, but it felt like there was; one of them murdering gunslingers, Keets or Brett, or maybe the pair of them waiting out there on the board-walk to gun him down just like they had Nate Simpler. Or maybe take him, lock him alongside Frank Gallons in the town jail to await their 'pleasure' when the mood took.

He shivered, blinked on wet, watery eyes and swallowed again. Damn it, they had shot Nate for no better reason than his being there. But why spare Gallons and himself, he wondered? They could have finished the whole thing, made a clean sweep, then and right there in Sam McAndrew's office. So maybe they had other plans, some scheming dreamed up by that swivel-eyed banker, Charlie Catches.

Like what? Hell, who could say?

Town was anybody's for the taking: Keets and Brett, some wild bunch riding back of them, worse still the O'Maras once they got to rounding up their strength. And if Sam McAndrew had truly died out there at Shelley's cabin . . . but maybe it was Sam who was still breathing and Walt Pond feeding the worms.

Whatever, Grateful was no place to be.

'Get back to yuh storekeepin', fella, while yuh got the chance,' Keets had drawled as he had thrown Frank Gallons behind bars. 'And think y'self lucky – for now.'

He did – oh, yes, he surely did – but what was luck if a fellow missed out on cashing in while it was running? Not worth a spit. So maybe the time had come to get clear, make a break for it before—

A noise. A footfall, somewhere out back. Damn it, the door there was still open. Should have locked it along of the others. Who was out there? Keets, Brett? Somebody moving awful careful. Somebody with a killer's step.

'Glad to see yuh still here, Ed,' hissed Gus Coles from the shadows. 'Thought yuh might've got to figurin' on leavin'. But yuh ain't, have yuh?'

Ed Murtrey ran his tongue over dry, cracked lips. 'Me?' he croaked. 'Leavin'? Why, hell no, Gus, I was just—'

'Lyin' through yuh teeth like yuh mostly do,

eh?' grinned Gus, stepping closer. 'Well, yuh can f'get it. Yuh started this, Ed, went along of Gallons and the others, now you're stayin' to finish it. Sure as fate yuh are.'

'Well, mebbe that ain't goin' to be so easy.'

'T'ain't, but that ain't to say some of us aren't for tryin'. We owe that much to Sam McAndrew, don't we? You specially, Ed. Unless, yuh want to finish up like Nate out there. He ain't for tryin' nothin', is he? Same might be said for Walt. Who can say? And with Frank sweatin' there in jail. . . . Well, now, that don't leave a deal, does it, savin' them we can round up?' Gus moved another step closer. 'But I gotta plan, Ed. Big and bold and sure as hell noisy. All we need is the luck to see it through.'

Luck, thought the storekeeper, just how much of it was there left on that tight rein?

Shelley Caister hugged herself against the suddenly chill night air, turned from the slow swirl of the shadow-streaked river and stared at the soft glow of lantern light at the cabin.

Sam McAndrew would sleep long and deep, she thought, the sleep of a man near exhausted from the fight with his own impatience. And when he woke, it would begin all over again, that same grunted reluctance to admit he was in no shape for much else save waiting for Walt Pond's rifle-shot wound to heal and for time to be the healer.

'Goddamnit, woman, I ain't never been one for sittin' out bad weather of the human kind,' he had snapped in his struggle to ease from the supper-

table to the cabin cot. 'And specially not when
there's a whole heap of scores to be reckoned back
there in that two-bit sonofabitch town. Tell yuh
somethin' else, I ain't never had no woman settlin'
them neither.'

'Yuh complainin'?' Shelley had asked, freshen-
ing the pillows at his head. 'Yuh weren't in no
shape to face Walt Pond.'

'Mebbe not, but that don't excuse. . . . What the
hell! Damnit, I owe yuh, Shelley.' He had sighed
and closed his eyes. 'Where'd yuh learn to handle
a Colt? Don't tell me! I can guess. Well, yuh can
holster it, yuh hear? You're all through. Retired.
My say so.' His eyes had opened wide and bright
and threatening. 'Next time there's any shootin' to
be done, I'm doin' it. Fact. And you stay well clear
of it. Understand?'

'Sure, sure,' Shelley had soothed, sitting at the
foot of the bed.

'Yuh wanna do somethin' real useful, yuh can
get y'self back to town come sun-up. Keep an eye
on them scum Charlie Catches has reined in. But
don't meddle none. Leave it to Doc 'til I'm good
and ready. Just watch and listen. No more. Keets
and Brett are deadly as a plague. Don't let 'em so
much as breathe on yuh.'

'How come yuh never mentioned Rockdale
before?' Shelley had asked.

' 'Cus it was way back and done with – so I reckoned. I was wrong. Should've figured for Wino and
Casey festerin' on comin' back soon as they got
free. Sorta vermin who cast long shadows. Hell,
what with them and Gallons and the O'Maras. . . .

Be a miracle if Grateful ain't wiped clean off the map!'

'Yuh don't have to go back,' Shelley had murmured. 'Town's brewed its poison. Let it drink it. Yuh could ride clear—'

'And leave Gallons wearin' the badge and Keets and Brett to spread their shadows? No, Shelley, yuh should know better than to say it.' He had sighed again and closed his eyes. 'Leave me a rifle, a horse, and you high-tail it outa here. Take Walt's body with yuh. Then just give me time. . . .'

Sure she would, she thought, strolling back to the cabin. She would give Sam McAndrew all the time he needed. Problem was, how long would he give himself?

Charlie Catches had spent the long hours of that same night watching time; staring at the hands on the baccy-stained face of the clock above the saloon bar and wondering just how long it would be before Wino Keets and Casey Brett reckoned they had soaked enough whiskey and fondled enough girls to call it a day.

Close on midnight now, he pondered, glancing at the clock again, and no hint of the pair moving from their table in the far corner. Might sit there till sun-up. Might insist on the rest of the town sitting with them, or until somebody got brave enough and foolish enough to make a move, the one that might see him stiff alongside Nate Simpler in Orton Grey's funeral parlour.

In God's name, this was going from bad to worse, thought Charlie, beginning to sweat. And

supposing Doc Lesters was right; supposing he
had recruited men whose sole aim was the
gunning of Sam McAndrew. Well, maybe Sam was
dead by now; maybe Walt had got to him – but
where, damn it, was Walt? But then supposing. . . .

The sweat on Charlie Catches' florid cheeks
had thickened to a streaky lather when the two
men hovering uncertainly at the bar over long-
emptied glasses made their move.

A nod between them, a quick glance at the
corner table, another nod and then the slow, shuffling steps away from the bar towards the
batwings.

Charlie swallowed deep on his dry, parched
throat as he watched the men go, his heart pounding, eyes swivelling from table to footsteps, mind
reeling through the odds of how far the pair would
get before Keets and Brett turned their attentions
from giggling girls and slopping whiskey.

Eight, nine, ten, a dozen creaking steps and the
men were at the centre of the bar, threading their
way through tables and chairs, easing like threatened flies towards the beckoning doors. Another
half-dozen and they would be clear, feet firmly on
the boardwalk then melting away to the night
with all the silence of shadows.

Charlie swallowed again, and promptly choked
at the scrape of a chair across floorboards, the
crash of a bottle, startled gasp from a thrown
aside bar girl.

'T'ain't that late, is it, fellas?' drawled Keets
coming to his feet.

The men halted, paused, turned flushed, quivering faces to the voice and simply stared.

'Yuh figure so?' drawled Keets again through a twitching grin. 'Yuh been watchin' that clock there? It troublin' yuh some? Hell, we can sure put an end to that, can't we?'

The grin faded as Keets slid his Colt from its holster and blazed two fast shots into the face of the clock.

'There yuh are – time's standin' still enough now, ain't it? Sorta timeless, yuh might say!'

The two men gazed at the shattered clock, gulped and eased a step back, their eyes tight now on the Colt levelled their way.

'You fellas stayin'?' mouthed Keets. 'Yuh fancy another drink? Mebbe one of these gals? Help y'selves. It's on the house, ain't that so Mr Catches?'

Charlie's smile hovered and collapsed behind a surge of sweat.

Keets grunted, grinned, strolled to the bar and leaned on it. His gaze shifted round the smoke-hazed room, to Charlie Catches, the cluster of girls, scattering of nervous twitching men, the two who had planned on leaving, and then to the floor at his feet and the slivers of broken clock-face glass.

'And speakin' of time,' he drawled softly, 'it's mebbe time this town and you folk here got used to the idea that me and my partner, Casey, are runnin' things from here on in. Yuh understand? Yuh wanna do anythin', go anywhere, say anythin' come to that, yuh do on our say-so. Clear enough?'

Charlie slid a hand over his sweating face. A bar girl blew a thin streak of cheroot smoke through the shafts of tired light. A man coughed, another scraped a boot. Casey Brett poured himself a drink, sank it and tugged a bare-shouldered, tousle-haired girl to his knee.

'Yeah,' drawled Keets again, 'seems like it is. But just so's there no doubtin' me and my partners intent 'til our business hereabouts is all through, there ain't nobody leavin' this bar t'night. Not yet they ain't.' His grin sharpened like a shard of the broken glass. 'And there won't be no shavin' t'morrow neither. Casey here shot yuh barberin' man a while back.'

Keets pushed himself away from the bar, holstered his Colt and straightened, tall and dark. 'Now who's goin' to get to tellin' me all about that one-time sheriff of yours, Sam McAndrew? And who's goin' to volunteer as hangman, 'cus we're stringin' up Frank Gallons come sun-up!'

Eleven

But nobody in the town of Grateful did much in the way of volunteering anything through that night. Few wanted to move, save when it was necessary and only then in slow, careful steps like animals suddenly spooked by the dark.

Those in the saloon stayed where they were, fearful, watchful, conscious of Keets's and Brett's every breath and gesture, one eye forever on the Colts that brooded black and heavy in the men's holsters.

Those outside, in the once safe and snug homes where life had always been hard and held together as much by the luck on the turn of a card or the seasons passing free of disease as by the effort put into it, sat cold and scared and wondering how they might slow the hours to the uncertain and unwelcome first light.

Nobody spoke a word that might be wasted. What was there to say that had not already been mouthed in the fever of fear and the shouted threats of the O'Maras? What could be said now that could be redeemed from the shooting of Sam

McAndrew and the panic that had brought Keets and Brett to town? And who had the guts to bury his pride and voice the fear they all felt, that if Charlie Catches' hired guns did not spill the blood, then the O'Maras surely would?

But every man and woman there through the silent, shadowed, empty hours asked questions.

Was Sam McAndrew really dead? What had happened to Walt Pond? Where was Shelley Caister; when would the gunslingers move again, what would they do; how would they do it, and would that be before or after the O'Maras loosed their rage?

How many wounded; how many dead? Who would be standing when Hell rode out, and where would their feet be planted – in a street choked by the smell of death or knee-deep in ashes? Maybe both.

But nobody that night was saying. Most were just praying.

Doc Lesters had his own thoughts as he paced as aimlessly as he had for the past two hours round his gloomy, lamp-lit front parlour.

The shooting of Nate Simpler had turned a new page. Wino Keets and Casey Brett had taken charge, tightened their grip, and there was no way now the town was going to shake it or them free, leastways not until they had come to a reckoning with Sam McAndrew. And it was there, in the fate of Sam and Shelley and Walt Pond that a deeper problem lay. If Pond's attempt to finish Sam had come to grief – or more to the point if Shelley Caister had raised the nerve to use her Colt –

then how long before Sam got it into his head to close the book on the events at Rockdale?

Damn it, it might be weeks yet before Sam was in any fit state to even think of leaving the cabin at Long Sands, let alone handling a gun. Could Shelley stop him, would she try, or would Keets and Brett get to kicking the dust from their boots and go find Sam for themselves?

Meantime, he pondered, how long before the town turned on itself in a frenzy of fear and recrimination and began eating its own heart? How long before somebody – Gus Coles for one, or Ed Murtrey – got lead happy and tried taking out Keets and Brett or even Charlie Catches?

And then how long before the hell of the O'Maras came pounding out of some sun-creased dawn?

Doc had paused at the window and stared long and hard into the shapeless night. Maybe he was counting out the years of his Fall, getting worn and knuckle-jointed where it pained the most, and maybe he had served long enough, done his job best he could, so maybe he should get to putting a finishing touch.

Something really useful, like opening the drawer there and getting the feel of that old .45. . . .

Ed Murtrey, on the other hand, had lost most of his feeling that night to a bottle of whiskey and the steady, endless drone of Gus Coles's voice.

'I ain't sayin' for certain it'll work,' Gus had muttered on. ' 'Course I ain't. Fool if I did. But that ain't the point, is it? Point is we're goin, to show them flea-hide varmints this town ain't for gettin' to its knees and grovellin' there for no man. No how. All it needs is gettin' started, and I got the means. Sure as hell I have! Now, yuh with me, yuh standin' to me, or yuh goin' to drown in that tonsil varnish? Sorta hand yuh had in all this, yuh ain't a deal of choice, have yuh? Might as well make amends with yuh Maker doin' somethin' useful as spillin' yuh guts for Wino Keets's amusement. Yuh with me?'

It was at that moment that Ed Murtrey's store had begun to tilt and swim before his very eyes and tomorrow seem a dozen territories away.

But, sure, he would stand to Gus Coles. Why not? The store, the town, his whole mangy life was all through anyhow. Might as well eat the dust here as anywhere and take Charlie Catches' rats with him, leaving nothing, not a lick-spittle, for the O'Mara bunch. But he would miss the girls at Shelley's Saloon, sure enough. Or maybe he would get real lucky and take a couple with him.

'So we'll wait 'til sun-up,' Gus muttered, taking a swig from the bottle. 'Them sonsofbitches won't be seein' nothin' straight come light – and won't never again time we've finished! Yessir, finest show in town, and yuh can bet yuh boots on that!'

But by then the heels of Ed Murtrey's boots were flat to the floorboards, the toes pointing skywards, and he was perhaps the only man in Grateful that night sleeping easy.

The silence that comes with a mist and haze-filled early morning had been broken by no more than

the occasional soft snort of a mount, the murmurings of midges, buzz of a lone fly when Shifty
Becks, long-time bar hand at Shelley's Saloon,
summoned the courage to creep through the flotsam of slumped, sleeping bodies, ease through the
batwings and take a deep gulp of fresh, liquor-free
air.

Was that good, *was it*, he thought, filling his
lungs, rubbing his eyes, scratching at the coating
of sweat-stained stubble, darn near good enough
to die for! And he might yet, he reflected, if either
one of them scumbags back there woke with a
nagging liver and twitchy fingers. Time of day for
a killing stood for nothing in Wino Keets's and
Casey Brett's reckoning. Any time, any place
seemed to be the thinking.

He sighed, stretched, yawned and shook his
limbs into reluctant life. Hell, for once in his forty
years he would truly welcome a bath; a tub of hot,
deep water and a thick bar of fancy soap back of
Nate Simpler's barber shop – save that there
would be no Nate this day or any other, no hot
water, no soap, no barbering and no shop open to
the street.

Dead and gone as its owner.

He shivered against the hazy mist and rubbed
the tops of his arms. Whole town seemed dead,
come to that. Nobody stirring so you would notice,
nothing moving. Place might be deserted. But not
for long, he figured. Not once Keets and Brett got
to waking.

He gazed down the long street to where it
drifted away to the empty, open lands. Damn it,

would it make his day right now to see somebody
riding in off that lonely trail. Somebody riding tall
and determined who might just have the guts to
take this town in a grip and shake it back to
sense.

Somebody, he guessed, like Sam McAndrew.
Sam could do it had he the mind. And always
assuming he still had a living body to go with it.

He sighed again and blinked. Well, no point in
speculating, he guessed. Best get back to that
filth-strewn bar and set to work, have it looking
something like a business for when Shelley finally
showed up. Hell, just what she was going to say,
and more than like do, minute she stepped—

Shifty paused then, blinked and rubbed his
eyes again. Night might have taken a rough toll,
sure enough, and could be those liquor fumes had
seeped into him like a downpour into a desert, but
unless he was seeing things there was a rider
coming out of those empty lands right now. And
more than one – no, hold it, one rider and a trail
mount loose-roped back of him.

Him? Damn it, that rider was a her! Shelley
Caister bringing in one very dead body. Had to be
Walt Pond. Hell!

But even as Shifty Becks took a step forward
there was a movement at his back. The slow,
squeaking creak of the batwings, the creased
leather pinch of a boot through a footfall, twisting
curl of cigar smoke.

'Well, now,' croaked Wino Keets, 'we got
ourselves some early company.'

Twelve

'Two guesses,' drawled Keets, lounging loose, arms folded, at the head of the four steps to the saloon, his gaze fixed like a shaft of the first sunlight on Shelley Caister's dirt-smudged face. 'One: you're a lonesome stray from somewheres bringin' in yuh pa to be buried decent. A wholesome daughter doin' her duty.' His grin sprawled behind a cloud of smoke. 'But t'ain't so, is it?

'No, t'ain't. So two: you're the owner of this saloon here back of me. And mighty hospitable too, ma'am. Yuh got my word on it. That makes yuh Shelley Caister, and *that*, the body there, must be the roomin-house fella, Walt Pond.' The grin sprawled again. 'Yuh shoot him, lady? That your doin'?

There were low murmurings, the scuff of uncomfortable boots as the gathering behind Keets pressed forward. Shelley sat her mount in silence, her eyes narrowed, hands tight on the reins.

'I'd say yuh did,' said Keets, skimming more smoke from the corner of his mouth. 'Well, ain't that smart? Real manly of yuh, ma'am, and no mistake. But yuh realize, don't yuh, yuh can't go about shootin' fellas as the fancy takes. That's crossin' the law, and seein' as me and my partner here are sorta wearin' the badge of it – temporarily, o'course – I guess we're goin' to have to deal with yuh as is fittin'. Yuh get my meanin'?'

Charlie Catches, his clothes crumpled, face still florid and gleaming with sweat, pushed to the front of the watching men and bar girls. 'Hey, now, let's not get to rushin' things here,' he blustered. 'I'm sure Miss Caister didn't get to shootin' Walt in cold blood, *if* she did. Why, I known Shelley since—'

'Yuh can leave this to us, Mr Catches,' snapped Keets, stiffening. 'Ain't no need for you to go frettin'.'

'Frettin'?' spluttered Charlie. 'I ain't frettin'. All I'm sayin' is how we just gotta—'

'F'get it, Charlie,' said Shelley with a knife-edge cut to her voice as she slid from the mount and slapped the dust from her tunic and pants. 'Yuh deep enough into this as it is. Don't make it worse.' She turned to the crowd of men. 'Orton Grey here?'

'Right here, Shelley,' simpered the undertaker shuffling to her side. 'Yuh want me to look to Walt here? Somethin' simple?'

'Simple as it comes,' said Shelley. 'And look to my horse while yuh at it. Horse comes first.' She swung her gaze to the huddle of dishevelled bar girls. 'You're lookin' like a herd of tarts there,' she grimaced. 'Go wash up, right now. Get them dresses cleaned and pressed, and then yuh take the day off. No more business' til I say so.' The gaze swung again, this time to settle cold as stone on Wino Keets. 'As for you, mister, whoever yuh are, you and yuh so-called partner get yuh butts and boots off my premises, yuh hear? Ain't nobody moves in on my saloon without an invitation, and I don't recall wirin' yuh one. So shift. Bar's closed.'

'Not so fast, lady,' began Keets.

'Yuh heard, mister,' snapped Shelley, her Colt suddenly tight and levelled in her hand. 'I ain't for repeatin' m'self.' The gathering of men and girls eased back. 'Go find y'self some other patch before I get to makin' shootin' men a habit.'

Keets's stare hardened. The fingers on his right hand flexed like tentacles. 'Why, sure, ma'am,' he croaked, the grin beginning to sprawl again. 'Still a mite early, and I guess yuh need to shake outa that trail dust. We'll get to this later.'

Shelley stretched to her full height. 'Don't bank on it. Fact, don't bank on nothin' hereabouts. We ain't in the business of a future right now.'

'What about Sam?' spluttered Charlie again, then began to blink behind more sweat under Shelley's withering gaze.

'Sam's just fine. Good as new. Sends his best.'

Charlie Catches groaned. Orton Grey began to hum. Keets's grin twitched.

'Now stand back, all of yuh,' clipped Shelley striding to the batwings. 'Shifty,' she called, turning, 'get this place cleaned up. Bar stinks. Open the windows. And somebody go tell Nate Simpler I'll be across his place for a bath in a half-hour.'

'Can't be done, Miss Shelley,' murmured Shifty. 'Nate's dead.'

Shelley hesitated, licked quickly at her lips, and shrugged. 'Shame,' she said softly. 'Guess I'll have to pour my own.' And then she removed her hat, tossed her hair loose and flounced through the wings like a breeze.

'Hell,' gulped Charlie Catches, 'now ain't that some woman!'

Wino Keets's stare deepened to a shadow.

Shelley Caister closed the door to her darkened room where the drapes hung drawn against the early light, leaned on it, sighed and shivered.

She threw her hat to the bed, unbuckled the gun belt and let it slide to the floor. Her eyes closed on the swirl of her thoughts. Damn it, she had run that too sharp for comfort. Another minute and that sonofabitch Keets might have lost his patience, but at least she had got away with the lies about Sam. Convincing enough to keep Keets and Brett here, she wondered, or might they fancy their chances and go find the cabin?

And just what in hell had been happening here? Nate Simpler dead, Keets and Brett running the show, Charlie Catches wallowing deeper into his own mire; and what of the others, Murtrey, Gus Coles, Gallons? She had best clean up and get to Doc, hear the situation from him.

Shelley was out of her boots and pants and unbuttoning her shirt when she heard the breathing in the shadowed corner beyond the window.

She waited, hardly daring to twitch so much as a finger, her eyes widening round and empty on meaningless space, her own breath tight in her chest. Somebody there, right there, been here all along, waiting for her, watching. And now. . . . She shivered at the sound of a movement and turned slowly to face it.

'Mornin', ma'am,' grated the voice. 'Figured for yuh comin' here soon as I heard yuh talkin' to my partner. Name's Brett, Casey Brett, long-time friend of Sam McAndrew.' There was a sharp intake of breath. 'But don't let me interrupt, ma'am. You carry right on. Don't mind me. I ain't goin' no place. Neither are you, come to that!'

'Get out!' hissed Shelley. 'Right now. Out!'

'Oh, there ain't no hurry, ma'am,' murmured Brett. 'We got all mornin'. Mebbe all day, eh? And don't go thinkin' on reachin' for that gun down there. Yuh'd never make it.'

'Just what the hell—' hissed Shelley again, buttoning the shirt with fumbling fingers.

'Now don't yuh get to latherin' y'self, ma'am. T'ain't good for yuh, specially not when yuh been so busy out there.' Brett chortled softly. 'Real busy woman, ain't yuh? Tendin' to my good friend Sam and shootin' up them as get in the way. My, my, yuh must think a lot of the fella. Hope he shows a suitable gratitude. But yuh know somethin', I also reckon yuh for a damn liar. I truly do.'

'What?' croaked Shelley.

'I figure yuh for a liar. Plain enough. I don't reckon on Sam McAndrew bein' in any sorta shape at all. I reckon you and him want us to think he's fine so's we'll just sit it out here waitin' on him. That it, ma'am? Sit here waitin' while meantime them O'Mara boys ride in and we all get to flounderin' in Hell?' Brett chortled again. 'Sure it is, and a good job yuh made of it. But I ain't so easily fooled. Nossir. So—' Brett stepped to a spread of dappled light. 'I'm for talkin' it through again. Civilized if yuh like, but I ain't to be trusted if it gets the other way. Know what I mean? Now, yuh goin' to see sense and tell me how Sam really is and how I can best go reckon him for m'self, or we goin' to have to fight over it?'

'You lay a finger on me . . .' croaked Shelley backing to the opposite end of the room.

'Oh, I ain't plannin' on fingers, ma'am, yuh can rest easy on that. No, I'm all for hands. Both of them. T'gether!'

Shelley backed another step, two, three, until she was flat against the wall and there was nowhere to go and nothing to see save the looming darkness of Casey Brett.

Thirteen

The smart guy breaks time like you would a wild horse and puts it to good use; the fool guy runs along of it and sweats. 'And you, Sam McAndrew, had sure as hell best get to know the difference fast if yuh wanna see yuh middle age.'

Well, maybe you were right at that, thought Sam, recalling his pa's long past words of advice as he winced his way another slow step from the cabin veranda to the edge of the river. Hard to say what lick of Mid-West wisdom his pa might have offered right now, but you could bet it would have come with a curse, a spit and a despairing moan. But, then, Pa had stayed a small-time rancher and never worn a law badge. There was a difference.

Sam paused, took a deep breath, hitched the Winchester tighter in his arm grip and narrowed his gaze over the breaking first light.

Another day, another chance to build his strength, find his feet, get to handling the rifle in his left hand and, damn it, discover if he had even the slimmest hope of staying alive long enough to use it. Pa might have had something to say about

that too, but he would have gone along with one
thing: Sam had to try, he owed it to himself, to the
town of Grateful and, not least, to Shelley Caister.

Maybe Shelley most of all.

Damn it, she had risked her life out here and
had probably laid it right on the line in going back
to face Wino Keets and Casey Brett. Neither of
the rats would blink an eye at shutting her up
minute she was of no further use. But Shelley
would be no soft ride, and with Doc along of
her. . . .

Hell, just who was he fooling? It was a tin can
to cut-glass that Grateful was a town torn
between despair and desperation right now, when
anything might happen and just about anybody
make it happen. The mis-heard word, a step in the
wrong direction and, whoosh, the place would
erupt faster than a hound on a bed of cactus.

And that would be without the help of the
O'Maras!

His gaze roved over the meanderings of mist
that clung to the river like washed-out shrouds
and came to rest on a lone twist of marooned drift-
wood reaching from the flow like a finger. He
grunted. It, that bleak twist of dead root, and Sam
McAndrew had grown close since Shelley's depar-
ture. It was a challenge, a target, the one thing in
this tumbling, jumbled sprawl of landscape that
had a purpose and a meaning.

Splinter that with a rifle shot from the hip, he
had told himself, and Sam McAndrew would be
back in the real world.

He had made a half-dozen attempts, every one

of them a miss; some wild, too high, too low, too far left, too wide to the right, and his pa's curses had echoed in his mind as if spoken at his side.

'Damnit, boy, ain 't nothin' to shootin'. I'm tellin'yuh. Take yuh mind off the piece, f'Crissake, and get to concentratin' on what it is you're shootin' at. Bring it closer. Let yuh thinkin' ease it to yuh like it was comin' to take candy from yuh fingers. Yuh can do it, sure yuh can. Concentrate. Make it move. Closer, closer. . . .'

Sam grunted again and, for all the morning chill in the air, began to sweat. Pa was right. He could do it, do it just like he had that day at Rockdale and a score of times since; do it for Pa, himself – for Shelley.

The Winchester slid from his armpit to his grip, the metal cold and mist-wet to the touch. Not the best of light for a shot like this, he thought, but, hell, he could find a dozen other lame excuses for missing if he had a mind!

'Easy now, easy,' he murmured, as his fingers felt instinctively for familiar shapes, the natural pressure. Get to thinking like Pa had said, bring that root closer; tighten the gaze; see nothing else; will the damn thing to be there, right before your eyes, as if it were asking to be smashed to splinters.

Just suppose it was Casey Brett.

'Yeah,' he murmured again, 'just suppose it *was* that sonofabitch!'

The pain in Sam's wounded shoulder came to life in a dull, steady throb. The sweat on his cheeks, across his brow, trickled through hot streaks, then, chilled, but his gaze stayed level, unmoving, unblinking, fixed like a beam on the twisted root that was now the shape of a man, the dawn-lit image of Casey Brett.

And then it was.

'Yuh plannin' on shootin' fresh fish for breakfast, McAndrew, or fancyin' a plate of fried toad? Either way, yuh ain't lookin' none too steady there!'

Casey Brett's grin spread like sand over his dirt-grimed face as he sat his mount loose upriver of Sam, a Colt dangling deceptively in his fingers.

'Good to see yuh again, Sheriff,' he called, levelling a long fount of spittle to the flow. 'Said to Wino back there in town as how I'd find yuh simple enough. The lady good as drew a map to yuh. Some woman, eh? Persuades kinda easy, though, don't she?'

Sam winced, licked at cold sweat, was conscious of the Winchester flat and heavy in his grip, his gaze beginning to swim and blur. 'If yuh've so much as—' he croaked.

'Don't fret y'self, McAndrew, that Shelley gal is still breathin',' grinned Brett. 'A mite bruised perhaps, but breathin'. Can't ask for more, can yuh?'

'Damn yuh, Brett!' groaned Sam.

'I'm sure yuh do, and some, but t'ain't of note right now, is it? What's done's done, just like it was at Rockdale, eh? Remember that? Sure yuh do – and me and Wino there, why, we had all the time in the world to recall. Ten whole years.' Brett's grin faded then flared again. 'Still, that's

as mebbe along with the rest. We got a reckonin'
right now, ain't we, and I been relishin' it for all
these long years.'

Sam stiffened, winced, fought for his grip on the
rifle.

'T'ain't goin' to be much of a fight, though, is it,
not with you all crooked like yuh are?' drawled
Brett, twirling the Colt. 'Some mess yuh got back
there in town. Yuh'll be best out of it, McAndrew.
Leave the flea-nest to the O'Maras. Me and
Wino'll be long gone by then. Mebbe take that
Shelley gal with us. Ain't got to know a half of her
yet, but what I seen so far. . . . Well, now, she'll be
real trail comfort for sure.'

Sam licked at another surge of sweat.

'Tell you what, Sheriff, I'll be fair, make this
fast, eh, so's we can all get to goin' where we're
destined? But I ain't goin' to have the time to bury
yuh decent, yuh understand. Time's pressin', and
you know Wino, likes things cut and dried real
quick and neat. What yuh say? Fair and fast, or do
yuh wanna go on fingerin' that piece 'til I get
bored?'

Sam blinked, swallowed and listened to that
voice still echoing through his mind.

'*Bring it closer . . . taking candy from yuh
fingers. . . . Concentrate. . . . Closer, closer. . . .*' The
rifle was easier now, hardly any weight at all, the
pain duller, the morning brighter. Sun was coming
up, clear into Casey Brett's eyes.

'I gotta busy mornin' planned, Casey. Wasn't
figurin' on no company, so I guess I'll have to
decline yuh fair offer and get m'self back to havin'

some space. Yuh do understand, don't yuh, but like yuh say time's pressin'.'

Concentrate. . . . Closer, closer. . . . Candy from yuh fingers. . . . Closer. . . .

Sam McAndrew released the blaze in a fury that seemed for a moment to rip that morning apart. He heard a groan, saw a snorting, prancing mount, the river stain red and the water leap like founts of silver fish, and then, in the sudden, empty silence that followed, the body of Casey Brett drifting slowly downstream, a dead weight in slow waters passing to oblivion.

He gave the twisted root a long glance and a soft smile as he turned for the cabin again, the sort of look he would have given Pa when Pa had, as ever, been proven right.

'Some candy!' he grunted, as he hunched the rifle to his armpit.

Fourteen

'So, yuh with us, Doc? Yuh goin' to stand to us? Only chance we got when yuh figure it.' Gus Coles hovered uncertainly at the window in Doc Lesters' front parlour, his glances flitting quickly from the street to the shadowed interior and the thoughtful frown on Doc's face, the anxious twitch at a nerve in Ed Murtrey's cheek. 'Time's runnin' out.'

'He's right, Doc,' murmured Ed, blinking his still blurred, whiskey-glazed eyes. 'We gotta make a move, and we gotta make it real soon. No tellin' what—'

'You fellas given a thought for the woman back there in my bedroom?' croaked Doc, pushing at his rolled shirtsleeves. 'Yuh got any idea what she's been through? Damn it, that sonofabitch Brett abused her to within an inch of her life. If I got any concerns right now, it's lookin' to Shelley. Ain't thinkin' no further.'

'But that's it, ain't it?' clipped Gus turning from the window again. 'That's the whole point. Brett beat the hell outa Shelley to get to Sam, and yuh can bet yuh sweet life that's where the scumbag is right now – out there at the cabin, and it's a hidin' to nothin' that Sam's breathin' days are done. Only a matter of time now before Brett's back here with Keets. And that pair ain't goin' to leave nothin' of this town worth the scrapin' up.'

'Mebbe,' frowned Doc. 'Yuh could be right about Sam, about what's goin' to happen here, but I reckon m'self lucky to have got Shelley outa that stinkin' saloon to my place without Keets finishin' her. Lucky to get to her while she'd still gotta flicker of life left in her. I ain't for pushin' it no further. Much as I can do now to stay with her, see if I can get her through the nightmare. You fellas do as yuh please. Can't stop yuh, but yuh sure as hell goin' to wreak some havoc with a plan like that. If you don't fry half the town, Keets and Brett'll fire it! Don't seem much of a choice from where I'm standin'.'

'Yuh gotta better plan, Doc?' grunted Murtrey.

'No, can't say I have,' said Doc, his gaze cold on the storekeeper's face. 'But, then, I wouldn't have gone along with the fever of the likes of Gallons, Nate Simpler, Walt Pond and Charlie Catches. I wouldn't have dragged this town to the brink it's sittin' on.' He paused as he made his way back to the bedroom. 'Yuh gotta lot to answer to, Ed. Just hope yuh got the stomach for it, however yuh do it. Now, if yuh don't mind I gotta patient back here—'

'Hold on,' snapped Gus, pressing closer to the window. 'What we got here? Matt Flankey ridin' into town like he had the Devil snappin' at his tail. What's brought him off that homestead of his? Matt don't saddle up to ride five miles for nothin'. Seems like he's headin'this way, Doc.'

The three men watched anxiously as the home-steader hitched his lathered mount, glanced furtively round the deserted street and scurried from the sunlight to Doc Lesters' shadowed front porch.

'Damn lucky Keets didn't spot him,' murmured Murtrey, wiping his bloodshot eyes.

'Bullet in the back if he had,' hissed Gus.

Doc opened the door to the sweating, dust-smothered man and ushered him into the parlour.

'What's eatin' yuh, Matt?' asked Gus. 'Yuh look as if yuh had a ghost sleepin' along of yuh.'

'Good as,' gasped Flankey, running shaking fingers through his sodden hair and then across his face. 'Yuh ain't seen nothin' like it. Nothin'. I ain't, and if—'

'Slow it down, fella,' soothed Doc. 'Easy does it. Ain't no point in rushin' the fence if yuh ain't goin' to clear it.'

'Get him a drink, Doc,' muttered Murtrey. 'One for me while you're at it.'

Doc grunted and poured a single measure from the bottle on the dresser. 'Yuh had yuh share, Ed,' he mouthed, handing the glass to Flankey. 'Now, in yuh own time, Matt. We're listenin'.'

'Yuh bet!' said Gus, standing at the window again.

'Started five days back,' croaked Flankey, finishing the drink. 'Noticed it out on the south drift, half-mile short of Old Rock, dozen or so riders passin' through like they had burrs on their butts. Didn't rate them none, rough-lookin' bunch, carryin' enough iron for an army. Gunslingin' drifters if ever I seen 'em.'

Flankey gulped, cleared more sweat, and blinked.

'They were back again same night,' he went on. 'Closer now and a deal more of 'em. Fifteen, mebbe twenty. Figured they might have an eye on some of the horse stock I got out there, so took to watchin' real close, day and night, rifle at the ready. Wouldn't have stood for no messin' – but they never came closer, just camped out there like they had no better place to go. Then I figured it. They were waitin' on somebody. Old Rock, my place, was a meetin' point. Reckoned then on gettin' to Sam McAndrew, but I heard as how. . . . Well, don't matter none, does it? Fact is, yesterday, close on noon, a whole new bunch of 'em rode in. Came from down south, and, hell, had they ridden hard. But worst of it, guess what?'

'I'm guessing', drawled Gus. 'The O'Mara's.'

'Yuh got it! The O'Maras, large as life, mean-lookin' as rattlers, herdin' that bunch of no-good-ers like they were generals. I tell yuh straight up, don't take no figurin', them scum are massin' out there – twenty-five, thirty mebbe – with only one thing in mind. They got just one target.'

'And we don't need no tellin' where and what it is, do we?' said Gus, his interest in the street suddenly abandoned.

'Hell,' murmured Murtrey, 'we ain't never goin' to stand no chance against that sorta onslaught. It'll be a massacre.'

'They still out there?' asked Doc.

'Still right there. Old Rock. Ain't moved,' said Flankey. 'But they will, sure as night they will. Could be anytime. Damn it, we just ain't goin' to know, are we? They're just goin' to come hell-raisin' into town and before yuh can so much as blink—'

'They see yuh leave?' asked Doc again.

'Don't reckon so,' muttered Flankey. 'Took the back trail out, real soft and slow 'til I figured I was clear, then kicked the dirt like the wind. They won't have noticed, not unless they get a fancy for my place, which they ain't so far. But mebbe that's only a matter of time.' He drained the dregs of the glass and shuddered. 'I tell yuh, Doc—'

'Yuh'd best get back, Matt,' said Doc, 'keep things out there lookin' normal. And don't go strayin' none. Look to yuh own skin.'

'And who'll be lookin' to ours?' croaked Murtrey. 'How we goin'—'

'Yuh gotta plan, ain't yuh?' flared Doc. 'Said as how yuh had. So yuh'd best get to sortin' it, hadn't yuh?'

'That's the spirit, Doc!' grinned Gus. 'Get at 'em, I say. Don't stand for no shyin' off.'

'And Keets and Brett, what about them?' clipped Murtrey.

'Brett's outa town, we know that. So that leaves just Keets,' said Gus. 'Somebody's goin' to have to deal with him before he gets to the notion of joinin' up with the O'Maras. Sorta double deal the sonofabitch'd pull once he sees the way of things.' Gus rubbed his hands. 'Well, Charlie Catches hired the scum, he can get rid of 'em, anyway he likes!'

'And when Brett gets back to town, what then?' said Murtrey, beginning to sweat.

'Casey Brett ain't goin' nowhere,' said the soft voice at their backs, 'not if what I heard yuh sayin' about him bein' out there at the cabin is a fact. He'll be dead by now. I know it.'

The men turned to face the bruised, dishevelled shape of Shelley Caister in the open doorway to the bedroom. She stood uncertainly, shakily, one hand on the jamb, her body shivering beneath the long nightdress, her eyes dark and hollow in their riveted stare.

'But Sam McAndrew ain't,' she whispered. 'Sam's comin' back. That's somethin' else I know.'

Fifteen

Charlie Catches licked his fingers, ran them down his bushy sideburns, straightened his waistcoat, adjusted his hat to a jaunty, devil-may-care angle, and stepped confidently into the sheriff's office, slamming the door behind him.

'You still awake, Herb?' he snapped at the guard, dozing fitfully behind the desk.

'Sure am, Mr Catches. Ain't closed my eyes in hours.'

'Nor should yuh,' huffed Charlie, swinging his gaze to the grey, stubble-shadowed face of Frank Gallons peering through watery eyes from behind the cell bars. 'Mr Keets wants to see Frank. Urgent. Yuh get them keys there, Herb, and unlock that door.'

'Well, ain't nobody said nothin' to me—' began Herb.

'I'm tellin' yuh,' said Charlie, his chest bulging as he tugged again at the waistcoat. 'We got developments and precious little time, so just get to it, will yuh?'

'If you say so, Mr Catches.'

'I do, I do.'

Charlie watched anxiously, the sweat beginning to gleam on his cheeks, as Herb struggled from behind the desk, collected the keys and crossed to the cell.

'Got to needin' me, have yuh?' croaked Gallons. 'Figured yuh might.'

Charlie merely grunted as Herb slid the key to the lock, swung the door open and stepped aside.

' 'Bout time too,' muttered Gallons. 'Some folk round here got some big explainin' to do, and it'd better be good.'

'All right, Herb,' said Charlie, 'that'll do for now. You just get y'self home, eh, catch up on some sleep? Yuh ain't needed here no more.'

Herb slapped his lips over toothless gums, scratched his head and dithered at the door to the street. 'Mebbe Mr Keets—'

'On his say-so,' smiled Charlie, ushering Herb to the boardwalk. 'Yuh got my word on it.'

Herb was still muttering as he disappeared and left Charlie and Gallons alone in the office.

'So what's itchin' in Wino's pants?' said Gallons, picking up his gunbelt, strapping it to his waist then spinning the barrel of his Colt. 'Don't tell me he's gettin' spooked?'

' 'Course he ain't,' spluttered Charlie, wiping the sweat from his face. 'He don't know nothin' about this. Thinks yuh still tight as a tick here. No, this is *my* plannin', Frank, while we still got a chance.'

Gallons slanted his eyes through a dark gaze. 'That so, Charlie? And just what yuh got in mind now? Another fuddle-headed piece of schemin'?'

'No, no. Now listen up, will yuh? Time's pressin'.' Charlie wiped his face again. Casey Brett's left town. Gone high-tailin' it out there to the cabin at Long Sands to settle with Sam McAndrew. Whipped Shelley Caister into tellin' him where Sam was holed-up. But don't yuh see, Frank, that leaves Keets alone here. Ain't nobody standin' to him, not a soul. Now's the time to strike, get to him, get it over with and back to where we were.'

'And yuh want me to do the strikin'. That it?' drawled Frank.

'Why, o'course,' grinned Charlie. 'Ain't nobody else, is there? Ain't nobody handles a gun way you do, Frank. We all know that. Damn it, we seen it. So what yuh say? Yuh goin' to do it, now, while we got a clear run?'

'Right now?' asked Gallons.

'No better time. None that I can see. Keets is down there at the saloon still playin' about with them gals. It'd be like puttin' bullets in a pail. Fella ain't expectin' nothin', least of all you, Frank. Yuh'd do it in one shot.'

'And when I done it?' said Gallons, spinning the barrel of the Colt again.

'Why, yuh'd be back to bein' sheriff, wouldn't yuh?' grinned Charlie. 'Ain't nobody'd argue with that. And with Keets outa the way—'

'No, Charlie, I reckon not,' said Gallons examining the gun.

'What?' spluttered Charlie. 'Why in hell's name not? Yuh got it made. Damn it, *I* made it for yuh! Risked everythin' comin' here.'

'Did yuh, Charlie? Did yuh really do that?' Gallons turned the Colt through his fingers. 'Or are yuh lookin' to yuh own skin again? Or mebbe figurin' on Keets takin' me out, eh? One less on the scene, and Keets is in your pay, ain't he? Yuh ain't one for wastin' money, Charlie, 'specially yuh own!'

'No, yuh got it all wrong, Frank. T'ain't like that at all. If we don't do somethin'—'

'Think it over, Charlie, while I go see for m'self, in my time, my way,' said Gallons, levelling the Colt as he thrust it into Charlie's gut. 'And I got just the place for some quiet contemplation – right there, in that cell! Shift, damn yuh!'

Charlie Catches could only moan through a lathering of cold, clinging sweat as the cell door clanged behind him.

Shifty Becks swished his besom over the same patch of bar-room floorboard for the twentieth time and stared through the shafts of smoke and dust-streaked sunlight at the lounging shape of Wino Keets seated at a corner table.

Fellow was taking life awful easy. Too damned easy by a half when you reckoned it. But that was the measure of the man: self-assured, confident, a gunslinger born in the mould. Sure, Casey Brett would be back, he was figuring; sure he would have settled with Sam McAndrew, and sure he and his partner would be riding clear of Grateful come sundown. Or not, as the fancy took.

Well, maybe not so easy at that.

Fellow sat there much longer supping whiskey

and spinning out his energy on the girls there might not be a deal of him still thinking straight if somebody happened along with a levelled Colt. Might be anybody. Fellow he was least expecting. A nobody person. Sort of fellow who swept floors, polished glasses, served whiskey and was just plain damn all. . . .

Shifty silenced the besom and stared hard. Be fair justice, would it not, if Casey Brett came back to find his partner stiff as old boots? Fair justice for Miss Shelley and the way they had treated her. Fair justice for the town, the whole territory come to that. Fitting tribute to the memory of Sam McAndrew too.

So somebody should get to it.

Shifty settled the besom against the bar, wiped his sweating hands on his apron and eased steadily towards the door to the stockroom. He had a gun in there, an old Colt from years back, but dry and wrapped and snuggled deep in the crates and barrels nobody gave a second glance. Always figured there might come a day when he would find a use for it.

This was going to be that day.

He was within a pace of the door, had a hand out for the knob, when the batwings squeaked, a floorboard creaked and boots creased to a halt.

Shifty swung round, narrowed his gaze on the shafted light and stiffened in a chilling sweat. Frank Gallons! Now just how in hell had he got here and just what had he in mind? No guesses. It was written black as rain on dry rock across his face.

'How'd yuh do it, Frank?' grinned Keets, easing the chair clear of the table as Gallons faced him. 'Yuh squeeze through the bars or did some rat oblige with the keys? Don't tell me. That banker fella squirmin' again? Sure he is. Playin' any which way with the odds. That's Charlie Catches for yuh.' His grin barely flickered through his granite gaze. 'So what now, Frank? Somethin' I can do for yuh?'

'Yuh can just get the hell outa this town, that's what yuh can do. You and yuh partner. Yuh ain't wanted here.' Gallons's face darkened as he stood his ground, a long shadow reaching ahead of him, his hands loose at his sides.

'Well, now,' said Keets, leaning back in the chair, 'that's not quite how me and Casey are seein' it. We're gettin' kinda attached to the place. Nice folk, decent liquor, good steaks. Gals are obligin' enough and, damn it, even the beds are soft. Fella can't ask for a deal more, can he? So we figure we might stay on a whiles, leastways 'til we been paid. Seems fair enough, don't it?'

'The hell it does!' spat Gallons, beginning to sweat. 'I'm wearin' the badge here—'

'Speakin' of which,' clipped Keets, 'me and Casey ain't too happy about that. Don't seem to us yuh earned it, Frank. More like just took it, eh? So we reckon it'd sit a whole lot more fittin' on my shirt. Yuh reckon?'

'Over my dead body,' growled Gallons.

'No need to go that far, Frank,' grinned Keets. 'Ain't figurin' on killin' yuh for it. Hell, no. All yuh gotta do is hand it over, go get y'self a drink, take it easy. 'T'ain't no big deal. Way yuh should be seein' it. . . .'

Fellow would have been hard put to say exactly how much Frank Gallons did see in the next ten seconds, thought Shifty, still with his back to the stockroom door. He might have caught the lightning flash of Wino Keets's hand to the butt of his holstered Colt. Might just have been aware of Keets stiffening where he sat, might even have seen the colder, keener gaze in the man's eyes, perhaps the gleam of the barrel and the sudden, searing blaze of the single shot.

He would surely have heard the roar, Keets's tittering laugh behind it, the echo of the blast, and most definitely felt the rush of pain in his thigh as hot lead pierced and buried itself in the flesh.

And then, thought Shifty, Gallons would have known nothing save the agony, the rush of blood, of grovelling on the floor at the feet of Wino Keets, his hands manacled round the wound like limpets.

'Yuh goin' to need a doc there, Frank,' grinned Keets, stepping from behind the table. 'Bar fella here'll go get him. Just can't stand the sight of so much blood, damn it!'

Keets moved to the bar and poured himself a drink before settling his dark gaze on Shifty. 'Yuh heard me, fella,' he ordered. 'Get the doc and tell him to bring that woman with him. I'm getting tired of folk spreadin' themselves round this town like they owned it. From here on I want 'em here, under one roof, where I can see 'em. And shoot 'em if need be!'

Shifty hurried from the bar without another

glance at the stockroom door.

Sixteen

That afternoon in Grateful shimmered sun-scorched, hot and silent to a shadowed, humid evening. The street, for the most part, stayed deserted, with only those in dire need of moving daring to do it.

All, it seemed, were waiting, some for the cover of darkness and the strange sense of security it brought with it, some for a new day, however it might dawn, whatever it might bring, most for the unwelcome sight of Casey Brett riding back to town with his sickly grin confirming that Sam McAndrew was finally dead, all with the haunting thoughts of the O'Maras' threat and the terror, death and destruction it would surely wreak, and none with the remotest notion of where they were heading, dead or alive.

But there were at least four folk in the town who had a hellishly clear idea of what that night might be hiding in its shadows.

Matt Flankey had left for the homestead at Old Rock at a pace, his one concern for the safety of his stock and the hope he would stay breathing

long enough to turn them loose from the O'Maras
if it came to it.

Gus Coles and Ed Murtrey had slid from sight
to the livery, Gus intent on getting to his 'plan'
and seeing it in action, Murtrey sweating on the
prospect and fighting a severe attack of throbbing
head and shaking hands.

Doc Lesters had been all set to send Shifty
Becks back to the saloon with the message to
Keets that he could 'fry in hell', but thought better
of it at the insistence of Shelley Caister.

'We don't go to him, he'll come to us,' she had
croaked, struggling into her torn, stained clothes.
'Don't make no sense, Doc, to get courtin' more
trouble. Stay close and I'll make it. 'Sides, I ain't
for dyin' yet, not 'til I seen Sam ride in.'

Doc had not argued. Maybe now was not the
time to stand to Keets. If he had what he figured
for a full hand and was the only player in town, he
would be fixing to win at every turn, no matter
who or what the cost. And Shelley needed him too,
not least as the prop to hold to her belief in Sam
McAndrew riding into town. Or the shoulder to
cry on when they brought him in dead.

Meanwhile, Charlie Catches had long since
given up trying to shout his way out of jail.
Nobody was listening, nobody cared. But the day
would come when they would, sure enough. Oh,
yes, Charlie resolved, they would be paying him
full attention next time they were looking to
extend credit lines, but would he be listening?
That would stir the dust, and the hell with it! But
for now. . . .

For now, he decided, he would sit it out — not a deal of choice — and give Gallons and Keets and the rest of the town come to that all the rope they needed. Somebody was going to get hanged. Maybe, he had pondered, sweating fit to near drown, but just who was going to step up as hang-man? Keets, the O'Maras? And when they were all through, would there be a town left worth a second glance?

Damn it, did he care? Did he hell! He cared because it had been his hand that had brought Keets and Brett to town. And maybe before this night was through somebody, somewhere was going to get to figuring it. Somebody was going to come looking for a reckoning.

Charlie, it seemed, could only wait. What else?

And so it was, as night crept into Grateful, that the town slid to its hauntings and saw the ghosts of them at every turn. No man, no woman, was spared and each lived with a past that was all too clear. What nobody saw was the future, not even when, as the darkness deepened, a line of riders moving slow and silent stirred the dust a half-mile to the west, on the trail that led directly into town.

Two fingers tapping out a monotonous beat on a stained tabletop told their own story, thought Doc Lesters, watching the relaxed but worried slouch of Wino Keets at his corner place in the saloon bar.

The fellow was beginning to have his doubts. He was wondering right now, reckoned Doc, on just how much longer Casey Brett was going to

be; wondering why he was taking so many hours
to finish a job that should have been over long
back; pondering on what might have happened
out there at the cabin that was so occupying a
man whose particular mark was his ruthless
speed: get to it, get it over, get out.

And slowly, but surely as sand drifting to a
gathering storm wind, he was figuring on something not being quite as it should be. He was,
when it came to it, beginning to sweat for the first
time in days.

Well, sweat on, thought Doc, turning his attention to Shelley Caister seated stiff and rigid and
staring at the table next to him.

Whatever her pain, whatever the turmoil of her
thoughts, she was toughing this out, and nobody,
not Keets, not the Devil himself should he push
through those batwings, would shift her one mite.
Shelley was simply waiting, clinging like she was
drowning, to the one faith, the only hope, she had:
that somewhere, somehow, Sam McAndrew was
alive and breathing.

God alone knew what a middle-aged, wounded,
one-time fast-shooting sheriff could do single-
handed to change this situation, but if that was
your faith, stay with it and pray on.

Doc grunted as he glanced quickly at the sleeping shape of Frank Gallons. He had patched him
best he could, but fact was the fellow had lead
buried deep. Another day in that state, and the
big-time stride of a loud-mouthed drunk would be
a thing of the past. Gallons would be ordering up
a wooden leg.

Doc's gaze moved on to the silent, brooding gatherings of men scattered round the bar. Fear among them now, he reckoned, was not so much the wild whip of Keets's temperament, the crazy shooting on a whim of Casey Brett, but the dread of what might be lurking deeper.

They had heard nothing, seen nothing, of the O'Maras in days, and that, they were figuring, was not good news. Blessing was that Flankey had kept his head and not mouthed his discovery for all to hear. But the silence was almost as bad. Twitch of a fretful cicada might be enough right now to loose a panic wide as a stampede.

Doc sighed and wondered how it was that Keets had overlooked the presence of Ed Murtrey and Gus Coles. Fellow was getting slack, his sharpness blunted by that two-finger tapping. Almost as monotonous as the soft swish of Shifty Beck's besom at the stockroom door.

Shifty had a real pride in that patch, thought Doc, settling his hand on his medicine bag. Nerves, it was all nerves.

'Get a grip, will yuh, f'Crissake!' snapped Gus Coles, wiping a line of sweat from his brow as he manhandled the box of dynamite to the bench in the old hut back of the livery. 'This ain't no time to go gettin' yuh nerves in a noose. And stand clear of that door. Anybody get so much as a sniff of us up here and Keets'll be blastin' lead like there ain't no t'morrow.'

Ed Murtrey stepped back from the open door to the glow of the low-lit lantern and blew into his cupped hands. 'Gettin' chilled,' he murmured, stifling another shiver.

'What yuh mean, chilled?' croaked Gus. 'Night's thick as mud. It's you, yuh lump-head. Too much booze and no guts for what we got to do. Now give a hand here and let's get to it.'

'This ain't goin' to work,' groaned Murtrey. 'Yuh goin' to set half the town to flame, mebbe most of it. Hell, there ain't goin' to be nothin', not a stick standin'.'

Gus eased the box to the bench and leaned on it. 'So yuh got some better idea, have yuh? Yuh been seein' things bottom of that bottle, clappin' eyes on some miracle that's goin' to come ridin' in and save the whole damned lot of us? That what yuh been seein', Ed? Workin' it all out? Well, let me tell yuh somethin' – t'ain't goin' to happen, not no how it ain't. We're here, this is now, and if we don't get to fixin' things good and proper this night there ain't goin' to be no sun-up for nobody, not you, not me, not one spit of a sonofabitch soul. Yuh got that into yuh fuddled head? Yuh see it?'

'Sure, I hear what yuh sayin', Gus,' shivered Murtrey, cupping his hands again, 'but, hell, what about the folk? How many we goin' to kill? How many are goin' to get burned alive, f'Crissake?'

'Didn't hear yuh talkin' so righteous when yuh were all for pinnin' that badge on Frank Gallons,' scoffed Gus. 'Didn't hear yuh bemoanin' the fate of Sam McAndrew, nor gettin' to lift a personal finger against Keets and Brett, or standin' to Shelley and her gals when yuh were needed. Trouble with you, Ed, yuh want yuh meat both sides of the bone, and then some.' He spat into the dirt at his feet. 'Yuh want outa this, Ed, yuh go now. Get back to Keets, lap-dog for him if you want, but let them who's got the stomach—'

'Hold it,' murmured Murtrey, turning to the night beyond the door. 'Yuh hear that?'

'Hear what?' croaked Gus.

'*That* – riders, a whole bunch of 'em and headin' this way.'

Murtrey stepped into the pitch black of night, waited, listening, peering, then turned again to the glow of the lantern. 'We're mebbe too late, anyhow,' he rasped. 'Them ain't no trail-dusted herd-punchers ridin' in: them's the O'Maras!'

Seventeen

Shifty Becks had made it – simple as leading a thirsty foal to mother's milk, and all the rest from here on would be just as easy.

Nothing to it, he thought, permitting himself a soft smile as he slid the old Colt to the folds of his apron, checked that the crates were back as he had found them, picked up the full bottle of whiskey and left the stockroom. Now all he had to do was go serve the bottle to Keets, slip the gun from the apron and shoot the sonofabitch clean through the head at point-blank range.

That simple, that easy. He could not miss.

And when he was through, when the famous Wino Keets lay slumped in his own blood and the town folk in the bar were heaving their sighs of relief and ordering up a round of drinks, he would look to Miss Shelley, just like he always had. Hell, she needed proper rest, a proper bed, her body easy between soft, silken sheets, right where it belonged and looked its best.

He swallowed as he stared through the haze of sweat and smoke in the cluttered bar. Important now to hold to his nerve. No shaking, no sudden movement. Just slow and easy like he always was.

And he could do it, sure he could. Hell, no, not for himself – he was no hero, never would be – no, for Miss Shelley. Do it for her. She had earned it, deserved it. Fellows hereabouts would do a lot for Shelley Caister, but he, trusty Shifty Becks, bar hand with the whispering besom, would kill for her. Gladly, and more than once along of it if that scumbag Casey Brett showed up.

They said killing got easier the more you did it. Well, he for one was game to try. Damn it, might get to putting aside his besom for a Colt assuming, of course, Miss Shelley wanted it that way.

He swallowed again and gripped the bottle. Keets was still at the table, still drumming, watching the batwings, a frown creasing his brow. He sure looked vulnerable just sat there, mind wandering like a blind stray. A deal to worry over maybe. Well, his worrying would soon be done. Two minutes from now he would be worrying about the hell-fire flame he was facing. Could be death would be a welcome relief from his earthly concerns. Damn it, could be Shifty Becks was about to do him a real favour!

Well, like Miss Shelley always said, give the customer what he wants. . . .

And it is as certain as night to day that Shifty would have done just that, clean and fast and no quarter given, save for the hell that broke loose in the street before he had taken another step.

*

The bar hushed to the roaring pound and beat of hoofs, the snorting of excited mounts, the whoops and yells of wild-eyed, liquored-up riders, crack and crease of leather and eerie jangle of dancing tack.

Faces turned, suddenly grey and pinched, to the batwings and the dark street beyond. Some men simply blinked and stared through sweat-wet eyes, others gazed as if drifting into dream-time, at a loss to comprehend the breaking fury or only too well aware of the nightmare that had ridden in.

Doc Lesters came slowly to his feet, his eyes tight and narrowed, one hand still on the medicine bag, the other reaching for Shelley Caister's shoulder.

Frank Gallons stirred and moaned and fell silent, mouth open, sweat lathering his face.

Wino Keets's drumming fingers paused in mid-air, hovered and collapsed to the table as he stiffened, sat upright, then pushed aside an empty bottle, slid his Colt from its holster and placed it flat, gleaming and defiant in front of him.

Somebody murmured 'Hell!' A shaking man dropped a glass. A fat man hissed and belched. A bar girl backed to the shadows. Another tugged nervously at the shreds of her torn dress. A third fingered the bruises on her neck.

Shifty Becks lowered the bottle of whiskey to the bar, swallowed on a dry, stinging throat and slid his hands through the folds of his apron to the warm butt of the old Colt. A nerve in his cheek began to twitch.

Smoke curled, soft and lost as mist, through the lantern-lit gloom.

Somewhere a chair creaked.

The fat man belched again.

It was a full minute then before the pounding hoofs, voices, snorts and jangling tack were stilled and the first boot hit the boardwalk with the thud of a tossed rock, but only seconds, it seemed, to the sight of a tanned, grubby hand on the batwings and the piercing squeak as they swung open on the grim-lipped, hollow-eyed, dust-streaked bulk of Orrin O'Mara.

'Glad to see yuh waited up on me,' he growled, swinging his gaze round the bar. 'Nice welcome. Darn sight more peaceable than last time, eh?' He clanged a line of spittle into a waiting spittoon. 'Said as how we'd be back, didn't I? Guess yuh must have taken it real serious. So yuh should. Serious business we got here.'

O'Mara's gaze darkened and narrowed as it moved over the wide-eyed, watching faces. He gave Shifty Becks no more than a glance, Doc Lesters a deeper, longer stare that shifted eagerly to Shelley Caister, its depth eating into her as he flickered a soft grin and licked his lips. It moved on, over sweating flesh, black stubbles, red-rimmed, fearful eyes, lolling mouths, tightened again on the bar girls, and then, like a leopard to its kill, to the hunched, shivering shape of Frank Gallons.

'That's him,' hissed Fergil O'Mara at his

brother's side. 'That's the sonofabitch who took out Clancy.'

'Yuh want I should kill him now, Orrin?' drawled the blue-eyed, smooth-skinned fellow stepping closer.

'Not yet, Sean, not yet. He ain't suffered near enough.'

Orrin O'Mara's gaze shifted again, this time to the Colt on the table and the man behind it. 'Well, now,' he grinned, wiping a hand across his mouth, 'ain't this somethin'? Wino Keets. Ain't crossed you, Wino, since before Rockdale. What yuh doin' holed up in a heap of a town like Grateful?'

'Long story,' drawled Keets relaxing. 'And y'self? Sounds like yuh got an army out there. Plannin' a war?'

'Sorta,' croaked O'Mara. 'Yeah, yuh might say that, 'ceptin' we won before we got started, so now we're here to finish the thing, wipe this whole flea-bed clean off the map 'til there ain't nothin' of it. And no folk neither. Not one. Yuh like it? Your sorta hoe-down, ain't it?'

'Sure,' smiled Keets, lifting the drumming fingers into action. 'I ain't got no cut with this place. And that goes for the folk, 'specially some.'

'Yuh can get to tellin' me 'bout it while the boys out there have their fun. They've come a long way for it. Gettin' anxious.' He turned to Fergil. 'Get the boys started. Don't wanna stick standin', yuh hear? Nothin'. Shoot who the hell yuh fancy. Take what yuh want, who yuh want, but I don't wanna hear no breathin' savin' our own when yuh done. Got it? Me and Wino here'll see to this place.' His gaze settled on Shelley Caister. 'We got some samplin' to do first. Meantime, turn the rats loose, Brother, and hang that bleedin' scum in the corner high as yuh can, but not before yuh scorched him some. Get to it! Let's see Grateful burn! Let's hear it scream!'

Eighteen

He had heard it all – every pound, every roar, every beat, snort and whoop – heard it trapped like a fly in an empty tin can, and not seen a damn thing!

Charlie Catches was sweating now fit to float, soaked through from shirt to skin, oozing the wet like his inside had broken its banks, and shivering with it. Hell, he thought, he should have guessed, should have known the O'Maras would stay close, probably no more than a nudge and a spit down the trail, ranging in every scumbag drifter and no-good passing through.

And plenty enough of that sort crossing the territory these days. Only had to ride a dozen miles in any direction and first rock you stopped to lift would be hiding some skulking rattler, ironed-up fit to furnish an army fort, booze-lathered so that they hardly knew which day it was, disease-ridden and sure as tomorrow looking for the next fast dollar from some place where the pickings were as easy as helping yourself at a candy jar.

Well, this town was no two-bit candy joint, not while he was still banker to it. Nossir!

Somebody should have got to the O'Maras long before now. Somebody who could stand to them, read their addled minds, speak their low-dirt language. Sure they should ... somebody like Wino Keets and Casey Brett; *very like* Keets and Brett!

Hell, what was he paying them good money for anyhow? No fool invested in a pail of water only to watch it turn green. Certainly not the likes of Charlie Catches. No, damn it, he would have to get to doing something about that. And fast.

Hah, some chance sweating it out behind bars! Might as well not be here at all for all the good he was doing. And as for that double-dealing Frank Gallons and his fancy, high-flying notion of wearing the law badge round here, why, he was no better than the O'Maras. Out of the same mould when you got to it. And another thing. . . .

Damn it, why was he standing here ranting on to himself when he should be doing? Doing what, he wondered? What was he *supposed* to do? Breaking jail had never quite figured in qualifying for a life in banking!

Now he was getting cynical. No, not cynical – he was going mad! Just that. Not there yet, but getting awful close. Right on the brink. Oh, yes, right there. Just give it another ten minutes, five, unless somebody, from somewhere. . . .

'Help!' he yelled, the sweat swirling on his jowls. 'Help! Ain't there nobody out there?'

'How'd yuh get there in the first place, Mr

Catches?' came the voice from the far side of the
shadow-drenched sheriff's office. 'I thought yuh
said. . . . Don't matter none,' mumbled Herb.
'Lucky for you I passed by, eh? Figured town's no
place to be, not now them O'Mara boys have
moved in. Yuh heard them? I tell yuh—'

'Never mind the talkin', Herb,' spluttered
Charlie. 'Just get them keys there and unlock this
door. Fast!'

'Sure, sure,' said Herb, slapping his lips as he
crossed to the cell. 'But yuh ask me, yuh mebbe a
darn sight safer right where yuh are. Way that
wild bunch is squarin' up there ain't goin' to be
nothin' of this town left worth a spit. T'ain't
natural. Them's just animals out there. Fact is, I
wouldn't disgrace no animal with the name
O'Mara. No, I wouldn't. Why, I'd sooner—'

'Will yuh just get this door open, f'Crissake?'
snapped Charlie through a swirl of sweat.

'You bet, Mr Catches. I'm comin' to it, just fast
as I can. Trouble is, this lock here ain't been all it
should since Billy Ritts stuck a blade in it night
he jumped town. Yuh remember that night, Mr
Catches? I was just gettin' set—'

'Herb, the door, damn yuh!' snapped Charlie
again.

'Nearly done it, Mr Catches, nearly there. Just
a turn here, flick there, turn left, twice right. . . .
Yuh gotta get the knack of it, yuh see. Ain't no
point in rushin' at it trail-buster-like in a whore's
bedroom. Never get nowhere like that. . . . Got it!
There yuh are, Mr Catches. Free as a turkey to an
empty gun. Like I say, lucky I passed by. Wouldn't

have bothered, not a mite, save for my bottle. Ain't goin' no place without my bottle. Ain't an O'Mara breathin' who'd spoil that.'

'What?' sighed Charlie, standing free at the open cell door. 'Bottle? What bottle?'

'Whiskey, o'course,' grinned Herb, crossing to the desk to fumble in the bottom drawer. 'Look yuh, only half empty. Half full, way I see it! Always kept a bottle here. Never could tell—'

And then Herb dropped the bottle to a shattered, scattered mass of glass and trickling liquid at the force of a blast far end of town that rocked the sheriff's office to its foundations and clanged the cell door shut again.

But Charlie Catches was on the outside now staring wide-eyed at the ceiling like a swatted fly.

The explosion that demolished and turned Nate Simpler's one-time barber's parlour to a blazing heap of matchwood halted the rampage of Orrin O'Mara's sidekicks in its tracks.

Twenty or so mean-eyed, devil-minded men, the flotsam of the plains, the scum of the drifters and two-bit gunslingers, were suddenly straddling the street bewildered and confused, some thrown headlong from panicking mounts, some caught flat-footed in the full blast, some forced to dive for cover.

The O'Mara brothers raced among them like demented dogs, yelling orders, shouting curses that rose in choking screams to the night.

The saloon had threatened to empty in the sudden dash to the batwings, only to be turned back by the roaring threat of Sean O'Mara's guns.

'First man to leave is a dead man!' he screamed, flashing his Colts over the bar crowd. 'Yuh hear that? Yuh'd just better, 'cus I ain't foolin' none. Ain't fussed one mite to another killin'. Fact, I thrive on it! Now get back, the lotta yuh. Back!'

But when a lean, bony-faced, frock-coated man clutching a timepiece rushed forward to clear the boardwalk he was dead under a blaze of lead before he hit the street dirt.

'Same goes for the next to get homesick,' yelled O'Mara.

Another man moved, but thought better of it. A pot-bellied fellow at his side was sick at his feet. The crowd eased back, murmuring, sweating, their eyes drawn suddenly now to the lick and roar of flames.

A fellow with a handful of money pocketed it. A bar girl fainted and was dragged like a sack of oats through the batwings. Somebody began to pray. Nobody joined him, or maybe they never heard.

Doc Lesters had grabbed Shelley Caister and rushed her to the cover of the bar at the first blast.

Frank Gallons had crawled in bleeding agony into deeper shadow.

Shifty Becks had drawn the old Colt from his apron and promptly dropped it in the heaving tide of bodies and boots that pounded floorboards, scattered chairs and tables and sent bottles and glasses showering to crushed slivers.

And for a full five minutes then the town of Grateful shuddered and shivered through a shouting, yelling madness that might have consumed it in one blood and flame-curdling gulp.

Ed Murtrey, lurking scared to the bone and still shaking in the depths of his store, had been tossed head-first into a mound of bulging sacks of seed and corn at the impact of the explosion not two doors away.

'Sonofabitch, he did it!' was all he had murmured as he struggled back to his feet and stumbled to the windows fronting the street.

The fire at the barber's parlour had spread fast and furious, the flames licking like demons' tongues through tinder-dry timbers. 'Hell,' Ed murmured again, wiping a hand frantically over the dusty panes, 'Whole town's going up!'

He watched as O'Mara's men scattered in their confusion, regrouped under the brothers' booming shouts and turned their vengeance and bewilderment then on anything, anybody that moved.

Gunfire filled the night.

Somewhere a woman wailed in uncontrolled sobbing.

Men yelled and cursed.

A girl's fear cracked in high-pitched, echoing screams.

A hound moaned.

Horses snorted, whinnied, bucked and pranced. Riders fought to stay mounted.

Another explosion rocked the night, this time showering shards of glass over the darkness so that it seemed to those covering their heads against the fall-out that the moon had splintered to a million pieces.

And soon, as the flames gathered like red-feathered vultures, fire was spreading, crackling, spitting, hissing as palls of smoke began to swing and drift in thick grey clouds.

Ed had half turned from the window, suddenly aware of the flames already devouring the back room, when he paused, pressed closer to the window and squinted on the flickering, shadowy shape of Gus Coles scuttling through the night like some frantic beetle, a bundle clutched firmly under one arm.

'Damnit, he ain't done yet,' he croaked. 'Not by a half he ain't! He's crazy, gotta be.'

His fingers spread over the windowpane, tapping, then knocking and scrambling to claws.

'Gus,' he called, but was no more to the passing shape than flesh mouthing silently. 'Gus – f'Crissake! The town, the town, damn yuh. Yuh puttin' the town to death!'

But when Ed Murtrey turned again he faced a wall of fire that seemed to stare back in leering defiance.

And then he too began to scream.

Nineteen

'Burn, damn yuh, burn! Every last stick, dirt and dust and all! Burn!' Gus Coles slithered to the side of a building, wiped the sweat from his ash-smeared face with a black grubby hand, and began to laugh.

'Yeah, burn, yuh goddamn sons-of-stinkin'-bitches, and see yuh all in Hell!' he yelled over the flaming night. 'I'll show yuh, show yuh all! This town ain't for crawlin' on its knees, lick-spittin' to the likes of no O'Mara scum. Nossir! You want it, yuh got it. Just a pile of dead ashes time I've done. Then yuh can take what yuh want, sure yuh can – bones, fellas, just bones, and yuh welcome to 'em. So come and get it, yuh rats!'

He primed and set to flame the trails of two more sticks of dynamite and hurled them into the crowded street, waited only seconds to screw his face against the blast, then primed a third stick and tossed it gently, softly through the windows of Charlie Catches' bank.

He was gone when the frontage showered from the heavens like a thousand flaming stars.

*

Wino Keets skidded through a pool of fresh, warm blood, took a firmer grip on the Colt in his right hand and decided then and there to put a bullet through the head of Frank Gallons.

'Doin' yuh a big favour, fella,' he croaked, as the shot blazed and echoed over the saloon bar. 'Darn sight faster than burnin' to death.'

He smirked coldly through the sweat lathering his face and turned quickly from the body to stare at Doc Lesters.

'Same go for you, Doc?' he mouthed. 'Or yuh goin' to make a run for it? No, t'ain't in yuh nature, is it, not while yuh got that medicine bag there alongside of yuh? Kinda badge of honour, ain't it? Where there's a medicine bag, there's a doc. Just like sand to scrub.' He took a slow step forward. 'But yuh know somethin', Doc, I got a curious streak in me. Sorta pricklin' back of the neck, so's I get to wonderin' times just what an honest, upstandin' man of medicine really carries in his bag.'

Doc flinched but stayed silent, one hand sweating on the bag.

'Yuh goin' to show me?' asked Keets, a grin spreading his lips.

Doc flinched again and narrowed his gaze.

'No?' mouthed Keets. 'Then I'll just have to take a look for m'self, won't I? If yuh don't mind!' He thrust his Colt ahead of him with one hand, grabbed the bag with the other, snapped it open and scattered the contents on the table in front of him.

Doc Lesters' old .45 hit the surface with the thud of flat granite.

'Well, now,' drawled Keets, running a slow, thoughtful finger down the barrel of the gun, 'ain't this some surprise? Never figured for yuh carryin' a piece along of yuh pills and potions, Doc. Surprisin' what curiosity teaches yuh, ain't it?' His grin flickered. 'So what's yuh thinkin' here? What yuh can't cure yuh get to killin' – that it? Or did yuh have somethin' else in mind? Sure like to hear.'

Doc stood his ground, his arms loose at his sides, shoulders hunched, sweat and dirt plastering his wispy hair to his head. 'I bet yuh would at that,' he sneered. 'Well, don't let it worry yuh none. Looks like I'm goin' to have enough to keep me goin' right here, don't it?'

'I'd reckon so,' smirked Keets. 'Won't be needin' this, then, will yuh?' He picked up the gun, spun the bullets to the palm of his hand, pocketed them and threw the empty piece across the floor, through the batwings to the night. 'There now, that's a whole lot safer, ain't it? Let them as is goin' to die do it natural, eh? Meantime. . . .' He swept the rest of the bag's contents to a corner. 'Meantime, Doc, this whole place is gettin' a mite too rough for me. I'm for pullin' out. Oh, and I'll be takin' the lady there along of me.'

'The hell yuh will!' croaked Doc.

'Now don't yuh go temptin' fate no more than yuh already have.' Keets eased forward. 'Just step aside there, Doc, and reckon y'self lucky I'm in a hurry. Any other time and I might've—'

Another explosion roared across the night, the
flames and burning debris spiralling high into the
sullen, smoke-smeared sky.

A man groaned. A woman screamed. Horses
whinnied. Orrin O'Mara's rantings echoed
through booming madness.

'The woman, Doc,' snapped Keets. 'Now!'

Doc Lesters stepped back, gathered himself and
might have made a half-hearted lunge at Keets
had the barrel of the gunslinger's piece not
whipped across his head to send him crashing to
the floor in a crumpled, bloodstained heap.

'Damn yuh meddlin' hide,' cursed Keets, grabbing wildly at Shelley Caister and dragging her
across the floor to the stockroom door. 'Damn yuh
all!' he hissed, as he disappeared, the dazed, half-
conscious body scuffing at his heels.

Only then did Shifty Becks summon the guts to
crawl from the pile of overturned tables, retrieve
his old Colt and step carefully in the wake of Wino
Keets.

Fire raging out of control, townfolk in a daze of
panic and fear, O'Mara's men caught between
risking their lives in the sweat of madness and
wondering if they were trapped at the heart of an
inferno, mounts scattering into darkness, buildings collapsing, sparks flying, and the sounds of it
all filling the night and the ears of the diminish-
ing few still standing – that was Grateful as the
hour ticked to midnight.

Charlie Catches was one still on his feet sway-

ing and staggering down the cluttered street as
he watched in stunned silence first his bank
explode and flare to oblivion, then the sheriff's
office, Walt Pond's rooming-house, the one-time
saddlers, Annie Morton's fabric store, Billy
McHenney's steak shop, the deserted home of the
long defunct, *Grateful Press*, the huts and shacks
back of Murtrey's mercantile, until, it seemed,
through his sweat-flooded gaze, the whole town,
north to south, east to west, was burning, scream-
ing, dying.

It would be a silent heap of smouldering ashes
come dawn, he reckoned. Assuming he was alive
to see it.

Shifty Becks was another still standing, lurking now wherever the flames left shadows and the
space for a man to slip into. He had Wino Keets
and the stumbling form of Shelley Caister close in
sight, right there ahead of him, dragging their
way to what remained of the livery.

Hell, if Keets had thoughts of rounding up a
loose mount, he was spitting on a long wind.
About all he would find in the way of a horse
would be a white-hot shoe.

Then what, wondered Shifty? Would the sonofabitch abandon Shelley and make a run for it?
He might try, and he might just run face on to a
blazing Colt.

'Be a pleasure, Mr Keets,' murmured Shifty,
padding to a new patch of shadow. 'A real pleasure!'

Doc Lesters had found his feet again, but only
to stagger dazed and bleeding, as far as the saloon

bar batwings where Orrin O'Mara was still
raging, demented and crazed, urging his men to
'Burn it, burn it! Take what yuh like, boys. Don't
leave nothin'. See it to Hell!'

O'Mara's brothers pranced and stamped at his
feet like drunken bears, alternately gulping from
bottles, scattering lead, grabbing bar girls, throwing them aside, dragging them back, ripping the
clothes from their bodies, and screeching to the
raging night, 'We got 'em, Clancy. We got 'em for
you and we ain't lettin' go, you bet we ain't!'

Doc could only groan at the sight, at the images
already racing across his mind of what he would
find come first light. But he knew, sure enough, he
knew.

And he wanted then to vomit like he had never
felt or done before.

Orton Grey was sitting it out in the depths of
the night with his back to a rare stretch of broken
fencing still not licked by flame.

So, he was reckoning in his calm, calculating
manner, he might have lost the best of his parlour,
every last stick of it, but at this rate, with the
bodies piling up like blown sage, he would be back
in business – and bigger with it – before the week
was through.

Only trouble was, there might not be a soul left
breathing able to pay. And he might be among
them. And Grateful a forgotten speck on a faded
map. And the whole of this night passed into the
pages of legend marked 'Horror'. Unless. . . .

It was only then that Orton Grey got to his feet
and stared through the drifting smoke to the far

end of town and the night-buried empty lands beyond.

He was thinking the impossible as he shuffled away.

Gus Coles was reckoning he had achieved the impossible. Hell, it had been a gamble from the minute he had lifted the lid on that dust-licked box back of the livery. A wild, unthinkable gamble that just nobody had given a spit for, something that would never work. And he was not sure that it had, not how he had first intended, but, damn it, them O'Mara boys had far from had it all their own way. Nossir!

But now it was done, he figured, scratching at the hot dirt with his boot where he stood on the trail to the west, beyond the raging buildings, the flames licking high into the darkness, clawing over the night sky like fiery talons, the smoke palls drifting grey as ghosts.

He swallowed. Done, sure enough, but at a price, and if Keets and the O'Maras were still there, still breathing and threatening and killing, then, damn it, where did that leave the impossible?

Just how had they all got here? Where were they going? Where was *he* going?

Only one thing he could do, he reckoned. Only one thing to do. Somebody had to do it, same as somebody had needed to get to fixing the town.

Gus Coles had stiffened then, wiped the sweat from his eyes, spat the taste of smoke from his mouth and was two steps down the trail, back towards the town, when he halted sharply at the soft, scuffing pad of hoofs through sand, the slow, easy tinkle of tack, shifting of worn leather.

He swung round, peered into the darkness, listened to the sounds as they slid through the night like murmurings, narrowed his eyes against the bite and sting of the fire, and waited until the blurred shape hardened and took on a form in the glow of the distant fire.

Sam McAndrew – ramrod straight in the saddle, his shoulder wound wrapped tight, one hand on the reins, a Winchester crooked in his left arm, and his stare fixed hard and straight and unblinking.

'Sam,' croaked Gus, 'we thought as how—'

But the rider passed on without a word.

Twenty

Fergil O'Mara had lost his grip on the girl and now his footing as he slithered through a scattering of charred timber and ash and fell to his knees.

'Damn the bitch!' he snarled, raising an arm to shield his eyes against the glare of flame. 'Yuh ain't goin' nowhere,' he yelled, blazing a volley of shots into the night from the gleaming Colt in his right hand. 'There ain't nowhere to go, not in this hell-hole there ain't!'

He slithered again, cursed, came slowly upright and staggered on. 'Don't figure on hidin' y'self some place, not unless yuh wanna fry,' he screamed. 'And yuh ain't for fryin', gal, not 'til I'm good and ready.'

He halted, swaying, the sweat bubbling on his face, filling his eyes as he gazed over the shells of burning buildings. 'Just get y'self out here, yuh hear? Make it easy on y'self. Or yuh want for me to turn the pack on yuh? Yuh'll regret that, sure enough. Them fellas ain't for. . . .'

His voice shallowed to a croak, then emptied on

a rasping swallow as his arms hung loose and his stare glazed on the silhouetted shape of the approaching rider.

'Hey, you there,' drawled O'Mara, steadying a sway. 'Yuh one of us? How come yuh still gotta horse? Yuh been skulkin' somewheres? Yuh seen a black-haired gal, darn near naked hereabouts? Yuh ain't been. . . .' O'Mara squinted, wiping his mouth. 'What's with yuh, fella? Yuh got some chip bitin' yuh shoulder? What yuh starin' like that for? What yuh—?'

The Winchester in Sam McAndrew's arm blazed only once, a roaring blast that threw Fergil O'Mara to the dirt and ash as if thrown aside like a shredded rag. 'That enough hell for yuh?' he murmured, and eased the mount on, deeper into the blazing town.

'My God!' hissed Charlie Catches, squirming on his knees in the shadows. 'He's here. He's back!'

Doc Lesters tensed and eased himself slowly to his feet as the batwings at Shelley's Saloon were thrown open on the sweat and ash-stained, smoke-smeared and blood-streaked shape of Sean O'Mara.

'This ain't goin' as planned,' he snapped, crossing to his brother Orrin at the bar and grabbing a whiskey bottle from his grip. 'Time we pulled out.'

'What yuh belly-achin' at?' slurred Orrin, drink dribbling from his lips, his eyes rolling, narrowing. 'What's eatin' yuh? Yuh run outa gals or somethin'? There ain't enough of 'em? Well, go find some. Get the boys to go look 'em out. Hell,

Sean, yuh gotta whole town to y'self. What more yuh want?'

Sean O'Mara slammed the bottle to the bar. 'There ain't none of the boys about no more,' he croaked. 'Yuh hear that, Orrin? They've gone, scattered, high-tailed it outa that hell back there. Yuh seen it, yuh seen that street? We got an inferno, Brother, a hell's fire inferno. That's what we got, and their ain't no man sane who's goin' to step to it.' He grabbed his brother's shirt. 'Boys have gone, Orrin. Gone. It's you, me and Fergil now. Yuh hearin' me?'

'Scumbags,' slurred O'Mara. 'No stomach, no guts, that's the way of it.' His lips slanted to a loose, lolling grin. 'Still, we did it, didn't we just, eh? Yeah. . . . Took this town apart in Clancy's name, to his memory, Brother. Yuh know that? That's what folk passin' through this territory are goin' to say when they get to steppin' on the ash here. They're goin' to say "Clancy O'Mara died here in a town they once called Grateful – 'til his brothers wiped it from the map!" That's what they're goin' to say, Brother. Yuh made yuh mark in history, that's what yuh done.'

Doc glanced quickly from the men to the flaming street beyond the batwings. Maybe Sean O'Mara was right, he thought, maybe the side-kicks had taken their fill, the raging fire got too much for them, and scattered. Maybe there was nothing here now worth the taking. Not even a life.

He winced at the crash of timbers, the roar of a fireball racing to the night, the echo of a pathetic

scream, and began to sweat at the thought of
Shelley in the grip of Wino Keets. Hell, supposing
Keets managed. . . . But his thoughts were stifled
in the sudden lurch of Orrin O'Mara across the
bar.

'Go see for m'self,' slurred the fellow brushing
his brother aside. 'I wanna see this town burnin',
every last stick of it. I wanna see 'em all dyin'. I
wanna hear them screamin' into Hell!'

'Yuh should be reckonin' on that sonofabitch
Keets,' croaked Sean. 'Yuh figured where he's
holin'-up? And he's got that woman with him.'

'Don't give a damn about Keets,' drawled
O'Mara, swaying against a broken table. 'He ain't
nobody. He can go to hell with the others. And if
yuh so darn set on that woman, yuh just go get
her for y'self.' He belched loudly. 'Yuh want for me
to do everythin' round here, f'Crissake?'

Doc moaned and glanced at the stockroom door.
Could he make it? Would O'Mara let him?

'Well, mebbe I will at that,' snarled Sean, pushing himself clear of the bar. 'And when I found her
and got to seein' Keets eatin' fried worms, I'm
pullin' out. Yuh listenin', Orrin? Yuh hearin' me?
I'm out, gettin' m'self and the woman some place
cooler. Yuh with me?'

'Not 'til I seen this town burned clean to ash,'
slurred O'Mara again, staggering two steps from
the table.

'Suit y'self. I seen enough.' Sean O'Mara paused
and swung his red-rimmed gaze to Doc. 'Yuh want
this sawbones stiffened out? Don't see no use for
him.'

'Yuh leave him where he is,' drawled O'Mara. 'He stays breathin'. Goin' to stand as witness, the last soul livin' to tell how it was. That so, Doc? Yuh goin' to do that?'

Doc swallowed. 'Don't look to have no choice,' he murmured.

'See?' grinned O'Mara. 'Fella understands well enough. Man there with a sense of history. Right, ain't I, Doc?'

'What the hell,' snapped Sean impatiently. 'I ain't waitin' on no history lesson. I'm out.' He emptied the whiskey bottle, hurled it across the bar to smash against the stockroom door, then turned his gaze on Doc again. 'Reckon y'self lucky, Doc,' he leered. 'Me, I wouldn't leave nobody breathin'.'

Sean O'Mara drew himself to his full height, ran a hand over his lathered face, hitched his pants and settled his gunbelt. 'See yuh around,' he clipped stepping clear of his brother as he headed for the batwings. 'Headin' south if it interests yuh. And when Fergil's all through chasin' his whores, yuh can tell him—'

He had pushed open a wing, grimaced against the surge of heat and glare of flame, but seen nothing of a threatening shape in that mayhem of leaping shadows, dancing, plunging flames, hissing ash and spitting cinders. Heard nothing beyond the roars, the creaks and crashes, and was a single step on to the boardwalk when the flash, deliberate, close, at almost point-blank range, threw him back to the wings, through them and into a twisted, bleeding heap at his brother's feet.

Orrin O'Mara stared at the lifeless, wide-eyed body, the stream of blood oozing over the floor-boards, lifted his blurred gaze to the still swinging batwings, and began to groan, a slow, low, rumbling groan deep in the pit of his stomach that grew until it burst as if in a violent bout of vomiting to a roar that hurtled round the bar like thunder.

Doc Lesters eased back, knocking a chair to the floor, his boots crunching through broken glass, his fingers, wet and sticky, fumbling uselessly at his sides, and watched as Orrin O'Mara, sober and steady, hurled himself in a crazed frenzy at the wings.

The man had a hand on the doors, was leaning his full weight into them, the sweat glistening on his face like grazed lines of ice, his roar mouthing to curses as a deeper, ringing blaze rose over the sounds of the inferno he was staring into.

O'Mara's head jerked back as if on a string, his eyeballs bulging like boiling mud pools. Blood spouted. The rattling roar was strangled. His body hovered for a moment, slumped over the batwings, hung there, then slowly, silently, like a mound of grease beginning to melt, slid to the floor and lay there, one arm stretched to the boardwalk, the other twisted to a grotesque root.

'Rockdale,' whispered Doc. 'That's how he did it at Rockdale!' He staggered across the bar, side-stepped O'Mara's body and crashed through the batwings. 'Sam!' he yelled at the top of his voice to the back of the rider. 'Sam – Keets has grabbed

Shelley, f'Crissake. He'll try for the livery, sure to.
Yuh hear me, Sam?'

The rider merely raised his rifle and moved on.

Twenty-one

Charlie Catches threw aside the scorched, blackened fancy waistcoat, ripped the floppy bow from his neck, rolled up his shirtsleeves and ran both hands, palms down, over his sweat-soaked face. He breathed deeply, coughed on the surge of smoke, spat and blinked to clear his eyes.

Hell, he thought, now he had seen everything, the whole damned wagontrain of life, and right in front of him, right there, not a spit away.

God alone knew what he looked like, what sort of half-dead, half-alive, ash and dirt-caked demon image he presented, but, hell, it was nothing to the sight of that fellow – the sight of Sam McAndrew sat astride that mount, a Winchester barrel gleaming ahead of him like it was the Devil's fork seeking out its victims. He had never seen, never heard—

'Yuh see that, Charlie,' gasped Orton Grey, staggering down the smouldering street to the banker's side. 'Yuh really see that? I ain't never seen the like of it, not in my life I ain't. And I tell yuh, I seen some shootin's and killin's in my time

138

and buried the remains when it was all through. But that ... that. ...' He mopped a grey, ash-caked hand over his brow. 'Yuh ever seen a fella taken out like that, Charlie Catches?'

'No, I ain't,' murmured Charlie with a vague, lost glaze over his eyes. 'Truth to tell it, I ain't.'

'But, hell, we shouldn't be standin' here like this,' spluttered the undertaker. ' 'Course we shouldn't. We should be right there, along of the fella. Helpin' him, damnit. Least we can do after what it's come to.'

'Helpin' him,' croaked Charlie. 'How in hell do yuh figure on *helping* a fella like that? He don't need no help, f'Crissake! He's his own man, ain't he? That's our goddamn sheriff there! That's Sam McAndrew, and this is Rockdale.'

'Rockdale?' frowned Grey. 'What's Rockdale gotta do with it?'

'Long story, Orton,' grinned Charlie. 'Too long to tell. And it ain't over yet!'

Shifty Becks had lost them, damn it, but they had to be there somewhere; gone deeper into the splintered, smoke-filled depths of the livery, or maybe lurking back of it, waiting on the luck to round up a mount.

Well, Wino Keets could think again, his luck was right out and staying that way.

Give it another few minutes, five at most, and he, Shifty Becks, was going to settle this privately, his way, in the blaze of a Colt till the chamber spun empty and the cordite hung like a cloud.

Had to be that way. No other, not now; not after

all these years and finally washing-up, not a dollar
to his name and no more than what he stood in,
and Miss Shelley taking him on like she had and
never asking one mite of whys and wherefores.

Took guts for a woman to do that in a place like
Grateful. Real guts – so least he could do was get
to seeing her right, specially now. And if that
meant finding himself eating dirt when it was
done, fair enough. Just so long as that filth-bag
Keets had breathed his last and Miss Shelley
could get back to. . . .

Hell, he hoped the next fellow swishing that
besom for her knew what he was about! Darn
sight more to a besom than most got to reckoning.

Shifty swallowed and took a firmer grip on the
Colt. Beginning to feel like a lead weight in his
hand. Wet with it too. Heck, them gunslinging
fellows must have a grip like a lion on its supper.
How they ever got to. . . .

Just a few more minutes.

Only two as it happened before Shifty's sweat
ran cold on his brow at the sound of scuffing
hoofs, the gentle snort of a mount, crack of
leather, jangle of tack, and the soft murmur of a
voice that ordered:

'Stand aside, Shifty. This is my show.'

Shifty took a painful twenty seconds to find the
muscles to move his legs; another ten to creep
from the shadow of his cover, glance quickly into
the cold, fixed stare of the man sat tall on the
mount, a Winchester crooked tight in his left arm,
and ease away from the brooding darkness of the
livery.

He said nothing, and could only swallow on a throat as dry as the drifting ash on the hot night air.

Charlie Catches and Orton Grey had struggled and stumbled like scorched spiders through the smouldering debris of the street, dodging the collapse of charred, blackened timbers, the sudden surges of rogue flame, stepping clear of bodies, the scatterings of goods and chattels, broken glass and glowing embers, to stand silent and sweating well short of the livery, their eyes fixed on the silhouetted shape of rider and mount.

Gus Coles had sweated his way to the saloon, seen Doc Lesters swaying on the blood-smeared boardwalk like a man in a deep sleep-walk, his face ashen and drawn, eyes hollowed, lips cracked, and hurried to his side.

'Hell, Doc, I didn't never figure for all this' – he swept an arm over the destruction – 'to happen like it has. All I reckoned was for puttin' some fear of death into these town numbskulls. Bring 'em to their senses. Hell, I never figured a few sticks of dynamite would get to this.'

'It's done, ain't it?' said Doc, shaking himself to reality, wiping the sweat from his neck. 'I gotta get busy, and I'm goin' to need help, all I can get. I'm goin' to need water, plenty of it, bandages. Hell, I'm goin' to need a miracle!'

'We should go help Sam,' spluttered Gus. 'He's here, right here in town. I seen him.'

'So have the O'Maras,' snapped Doc. 'For the last time!'

'But, heck, Doc, there's Keets and Miss Shelley. If Wino's got his hands on her. . . . Hell! Sam ain't in no shape to go on killin', is he? And that fella is sharper than a rattler with toothache when it comes to handlin' a Colt. I wouldn't give a—'

'Know somethin', Gus?' said Doc, throwing aside his jacket, rolling up his shirtsleeves. 'Last thing troublin' me right now is Wino Keets. Yuh ever heard of a town called Rockdale?'

'No, can't say I have.'

'Pity,' grunted Doc. 'Yuh'd know what to expect if yuh had. Now, yuh goin' to get busy along of me here, or stand catchin' ash in that open mouth? Water, bandages . . . let's keep alive what there is left of this town.' He stared into the flame-lit night. 'Sam McAndrew'll do the rest.'

Twenty-two

'All yuh gotta do is watch, and stay calm enough
to be watched. That's how yuh get to makin' a kill
– of any sort.'

That had been Pa with his nose to the track and
supper in sight, thought Sam, tightening the rein
against the mount's twitch, but that had been at
a slow, warm, sunlit dusk in the long blue grass
with only a jack-rabbit's stiff, silky ears to watch.

That had not been here, in a flaming hell with
a dozen shadows staring back and any one of
them set to loose a blaze of lead.

And Wino Keets was no jack-rabbit.

Right now he was as near as damn it stifling
the life out of Shelley Caister to keep her silence,
weighing the odds, seeing all the angles, every
twist and turn of every escape route, figuring just
how and when he was going to get his hands on
McAndrew's horse.

Figuring, too, that he had seen the last of Casey
Brett and the O'Mara brothers – and maybe
Charlie Catches and his money trough – and that
the fellow seated out there, a flaming town back of

143

him, the stench of death and ash, smoke and
cordite filling the air fit to choke on, was a ghost
from a past that had been trailing the pair of
them all the way from Rockdale.

Sam settled the mount again and waited, the
rifle easy in his grip, the sweat soft at his neck,
across his brow, his gaze moving slow as a beam
over the livery shadows.

All it needed was a single movement, something as simple as the twitch of a shoulder – or for
Shelley, damn it, to struggle just one more time.

'Hell, I figure for Keets holdin' Shelley in the
livery there and Sam's a sittin' target,' murmured
Charlie Catches, blinking and sniffing against a
drift of smoke. 'All it'd need is for Keets to level a
Colt. Just one shot.' He swallowed. 'Mebbe we
should get to flushin' out that sonofabitch. What
yuh say, Orton? We go do that? Give Sam a hand
there?'

'No,' croaked the undertaker. 'This ain't for our
meddlin'.'

'Meddlin', f'Crissake!' blustered Charlie. 'What
we got back of us? What's this hell-hole night if it
ain't meddlin? We been *meddlin'* since the day
that O'Mara scum creased the dust here. We got
to *meddlin'* minute we set Frank Gallons up on
that damned law-keepin' pedestal, and we sure as
hell got to *meddlin'* deep as it gets when Walt
Pond put a bullet into Sam there. That's the
meddlin' we been doin', f'Crissake!'

'Not to mention yuh own contribution,' croaked
Grey with a sharp, sidelong glance. 'Don't let's

overlook Keets and Brett. That was *meddlin'* and some.'

'I ain't disputin' my mistakes,' snapped Charlie. 'Not one mite I ain't, but, damnit, Orton, this is somethin' else. Yuh got the slightest notion how many dead we got now, right this minute? Yuh got any idea at all?'

'I'm countin',' murmured Grey dolefully.

'I'll bet yuh are at that! And there's gonna be a whole lot more yet, Sam McAndrew among 'em if we don't cut this meddlin' talk and get to *doin'* somethin'. I'm tellin' yuh, we done enough *meddlin'* to last this territory 'til doomsday.'

'What makes yuh think we ain't already there?' croaked Grey again.

Shifty Becks was shivering now, the sweat on his back like mountain creek water, his hands fidgeting and shaking over the old Colt still buried deep in the folds of his apron.

He should get to using it, right now, he thought, before Keets made his move. Fire a shot into any one of the shadows. Might not be the right one, but did it matter? Keets would move, sure enough, would have to, pure instinct, and that might give Sam the edge, just the chance he wanted.

But supposing he hit Miss Shelley? Supposing that! Hell, it would all be a waste. So maybe better to wait, let Sam have it his way. Wait, here in the dirt and the ash and the heat of the flames. Just wait. After all, if there was anybody hereabouts who knew what they were doing, it had to

be Sam McAndrew. He might be marking up the
years, but when it came to holding to the law as
sheriff and handling a Colt, town had never seen
finer.

Pity some folk had not reckoned that a few days
back – long before they not only got to losing their
sheriff, but the town along of him.

Shifty winced and ducked instinctively at the
crash, roar and splinter of another building
collapsing under the lick of flames. Hell, how
much more, how much longer? And then he stiffened and swallowed at what he was certain was a
movement in the shadows out there.

No wonder a fellow got to shivering.

But had Sam seen the same movement?

Sam had seen it, sure enough, just the faintest
swish of light in the shadow far to his left. That
would have been Shelley, he reckoned, summon-
ing all the strength in her drained body to struggle against Keets one more time. Now she would
stay quiet, trusting that Sam had pinpointed
Keets's cover, that his nerve would hold and Wino
begin to crack.

Sam eased the mount a shade to the left to
bring it head-on to where Keets lay hidden, eased
his grip on the Winchester sufficient to flex his
fingers and take a new hold. His gaze tightened,
narrowed, shutting out everything save the patch
of shadow.

He licked his lips, stiffened, same as he had
that day back in Rockdale, same as Pa had always

said: 'Tain't the waitin', boy, it's the spine-bendin'
watchin'!'

'That it, McAndrew? That as far as yuh comin?'
called Keets. 'Yuh should know I got yuh plumb in
my sights. Don't look healthy. Best get to it. T'ain't
a night for lingerin' on.'

Sam stiffened again, held the narrowed gaze,
waited for another movement, the certainty now
that any attempt to take out Keets would not end
in the slumped, lead-blasted body of Shelley
Caister.

'I see yuh, Wino,' he grunted, licking at more
sweat.

'Oh, now, I doubt that for a fact,' mocked Keets.
'Yuh seein' what yuh wanna see, McAndrew, not a
deal more. Tell yuh what yuh ain't seein: yuh ain't
seein' this woman I got here. Just outa yuh sight,
ain't she? One loose finger on that Winchester yuh
probin' there and yuh could make one helluva
mess of her pretty body, couldn't yuh? Yuh
thought of that, McAndrew? Yuh should.'

Sam shifted the rifle a touch to the right. Damn
the fellow's mangy hide! He was right, there was
no target.

Not yet.

'So I figure on us doin' a deal on this,' called
Keets again. 'Yuh listening, Law-keeper?'

'No deal,' grunted Sam. 'Same as there weren't
for yuh sidekick, and none for the O'Maras
neither.'

'Yuh been busy, McAndrew. Just like yuh
always were, eh? Real busy fella. But this ain't the
same, is it? Yuh gotta think this through real

thorough. Looks like yuh lost most of yuh two-bit town, don't it, so yuh'd best not get real careless and add this lady here to the Boot Hill party. What yuh say, we gotta deal here: that good-lookin' horse of yours for this pretty woman and we all stay breathin'? Seems fair from where I'm standing, and if it don't from where you are, then yuh one helluva dumb fool, McAndrew. Now, what yuh say, we dealin'?'

'Comes a time when it's all down to bluff,' had been Pa's figuring out there in the blue grass. *'Sure it does. That jack-rabbit sittin' there's reck-onin' on how he might just get to starin' yuh out, stayin' that mite far side of yuh range and figurin' yuh ain't for movin'. Now, question is, who's bluf-fin' who? That's what yuh gotta decide, boy.'*

'See yuh in hell first!' snapped Sam, tightening the rein, gripping the Winchester.

'Oh, my, ain't you just one sonofabitch stubborn critter? Don't change one bit, do yuh? Just like Rockdale, eh? Yuh recall that, McAndrew? Sure yuh do. Clear as if it were yesterday, I bet. Yuh standin' there to the Peterson boys, me and Casey along of 'em. Yuh sure got stubborn that day. Oh, my, did you!'

'Longer he can keep yuh starin', boy, better chance he's got of givin' yuh the slip. . . .'

'I remember,' called Sam, his stare narrowing and squinting for another movement. 'Didn't come outa that too well neither, did yuh? Got to over-playin' yuh hand as I recall.'

'Luck, all down to luck,' sneered Keets. 'Not been for that nosyin' kid crossin' the street, yuh'd have been sniffin' dirt, McAndrew.'

'Who's to say I didn't get the kid to cross the street? Yuh thought of that, Wino?' mocked Sam. 'Mebbe yuh just fell for the oldest trick goin', eh? Careless thinkin', I'd reckon.'

'Yuh sayin' as how—'

'Yuh ain't never goin' to know, are yuh?'

Had Keets moved, wondered Sam, had the voice shifted a shade to the left? Hard to tell; difficult to be certain.

'*So what yuh really gotta do, boy, is keep watchin' and figurin' for just where the critter's plannin' a bolt-hole.*'

'Mebbe I should've shot the kid, eh?' sneered Keets again. 'What would yuh've done then, McAndrew? Takin' an awful risk there, weren't yuh?'

'Everythin's a risk, Wino. Whole world's just one big risk. Yuh born to it, yuh risk it. Way of things, ain't it?'

'Don't get to no smart talkin' me, damn yuh. It ain't goin' to work.'

Sam stiffened. The voice had moved.

'*And sooner or later, boy, one of yuh's goin' to have to take the risk. . . .*'

'Sam! On yuh left!' screamed Shelley Caister scrambling on all-fours from the shadow to the dirt.

The mount bucked, lifting Sam and the rifle aim to the right as Keets plunged from the darkness to stand, half-crouched, legs parted, his Colt already blazing against the glow of the burning town and seeping slivers of smoke.

Sam crashed to the ground, the impact sending a searing stab of pain through the wounded shoulder, spinning the Winchester from his grip.

'Sam!' screamed Shelley again, grovelling towards him.

Keets's laughter rose screeching and echoing over the night, his lips curling, eyes flashing, the Colt blazing on. 'Yuh had yuh chance, McAndrew. Should've taken it,' he snarled. 'Too late now, damn yuh. Too late!'

Sam scrambled through the dirt and ash, blinded now by smoke, the spiralling dust, in one lunge crashing against the panicking mount, in the next reaching into space for Shelley.

Nothing, only the dirt and the closing shape of Keets as he stepped slow and steady for the final shot. Shelley screamed again, clawing madly for a grip on Keets's legs. Sam rolled clear of the horse, desperate now for the shadows, for a chance to scramble for the grounded rifle.

He scooped a handful of ash and hurled it high and wide, scrambled again. Cover, he needed cover. Keets fired again, this time spooking the mount to a frenzy as it rose on its hindlegs, snorting and pawing on the cloud of ash.

Sam threw himself backwards, then to the right, his knee crashing against a smouldering timber. He winced, squirmed on, hurled more dirt, and was staggering to his feet when the Colt landed at his feet with a defiant thud.

'Grab it, Sam!' yelled Shifty Becks, straddling the higher ground at McAndrew's back, the folds of his dirt-smeared apron wrapped round his legs like twisted wings. 'Grab it!'

Sam reached, grabbed with his left hand, struggled upright, blood coursing from the shoulder wound, his face caked with ash, eyes gleaming through it like blazing coals, swung round and released the roaring power of Shifty's storeroom Colt.

Wino Keets staggered, swayed, ran a hand through a surge of blood across his chest, staggered again, grinned on twisting, twitching lips, rolled his eyes and hit the dirt face-down, his gun still tight in his fingers.

And in the moments that followed, as Charlie Catches, Orton Grey and Gus Coles simply stared in silence, Shelley Caister sobbed, Shifty Becks let tears of pride roll warm and free, and Sam McAndrew stood alone, the town of Grateful gasped its last in a splintering, shuddering mass and crash of flaming timber.

And the heavens burned too, some said.

Twenty-three

There were ten days or more – nobody was much for counting – following that night when the skeletal remains, the dead, blackened bones and scorched, hanging flesh of what had once been a town, lay as silent as the grave.

Not surprising, thought Gus Coles, struggling as he had for the past week to bring some sort of order to the chaos of his one-time livery. Grateful was a grave, just one big, awesome Boot Hill, the deepest west of Denver.

And it only needed a glance to confirm it.

Sure, there was still a street out there, dark as a skim of dried blood, ankle-deep in ash and cinders, cluttered and splattered with the gruesome flotsam of fire. And, sure, there was still something standing: stiff, flame-chewed timbers lifting like old fingers to the clear blue Mid-West sky; the door to Nate Simpler's barber shop closed tight shut on empty space; the floor of Ed Murtrey's store; half of the back wall of Walt Pond's rooming-house, the twisted frame of an iron bed at rest against it; only the bars and cell door of the jail; nothing of the bank save ashes; nothing of Doc Lesters' surgery and home; not so much as a pine plank of the funeral parlour; most houses burned to the ground, and just enough of Shelley Caister's saloon to make it the pathetic heart of sad remains.

The saloon had become Doc's surgery, the town feeding-house and water supply from its outback well, a vast bazaar of anything and everything that was still usable; a place where folk could sleep, and weep, and find what comfort there was when the dead had been buried, decent as was possible, and the living left to figure if the future too had not died with them.

'Not in my book it ain't,' Gus had told Doc Lesters. 'But, then, I gotta say that, ain't I? Damn it, who was it started this whole thing? Who was it threw that first stick of dynamite?'

'Town did,' Doc had answered. 'Threw it the night it pinned the badge of law on Frank Gallons's shirt, turned its back on sense and logic and whipped itself to a frenzy of fear and hate and rode full rein for Hell. That was the "dynamite" and the flames were the likes of Pond and Murtrey, Nate Simpler and a banker who figured his money could buy the peace.'

Well, thought Gus, scratching his head as he fathomed just how much of the stabling he could save, maybe Doc was right, maybe that night of the shooting of Sam McAndrew had been the start.

Certainly Charlie Catches reckoned so.

'Hell, we just never stopped to listen, did we?

No way. We spooked ourselves fit to vomit with
the O'Maras, and then, damn it, who's the mule-
head who goes bringin' in the guns, buyin' em like
they were so many beans in a mangy sack? Why,
me, o'course!' he had spluttered. 'Good old Charlie
Catches! And now, I ain't got so much as the door
to a bank, let alone a bank!'

That was true enough Shelley Caister had
agreed, looking Charlie straight in the eye. 'Yuh
ain't got no home neither,' she had told him,
rummaging through a rescued chest of clothes for
anything that was still in one piece and might fit
the girls and women gathered round her. 'But yuh
sure as night got one thing in hellish short supply
round here: yuh got the *means* to gettin' yuh
hands on money, ain't yuh? Yuh still a *banker*,
aren't yuh? That ain't changed none. So yuh know
just what yuh gotta do, don't yuh, Charlie?'

Did he? Damn it, he was game for anything if it
would help. Only decent thing he could do. Not, of
course, that he had ever intended for Wino Keets
and Casey Brett to turn out the way they had, and
not that he could have known, could he, about
Rockdale, the Peterson gang and Sam
McAndrew's part in settling the issue back there.
Even so, a banker's word and honour were at
stake here, not to mention the town's future, so if
there was anything, anything at all, he could
do. . . .

'Sure, sure,' Shelley had soothed impatiently,
her hands set tight on her hips, her girls round
her like a waiting brood, the leftovers of the chest
of clothes scattered at her feet. 'Well, first thing

yuh can do is stop whingin' and feelin' sorry for
y'self and thrashin' y'self into a lathered heap
there. T'ain't practical – nobody can eat it, drink
it, wear it, or live in it. Got it? Right, then yuh get
y'self outa this stinkin' hell-hole by any means
yuh can rustle up and over to them moneybags
fellas back there in Denver and raise all the cash
– cash, mark yuh – yuh can lay a hand to.

'And no messin', Charlie. I mean *real* money, fat
as it comes, so we can all get to puttin' this town
back to somethin' worth livin' in. And some hard-
line investment while yuh at it. Men who'll put
their profits into folk, homes, stores, mercantiles,
business. That's what yuh gotta do, Charlie
Catches, if yuh wanna sleep easy come nights.
And if yuh don't, I'll personally put a bullet 'tween
yuh eyes! Oh, and go easy on the fancy waistcoats.
Buy some fabrics for the ladies here. Got it,
Charlie? Now go redeem y'self before we change
our minds and get to shootin' yuh, anyhow!'

Charlie would at that, thought Gus, turning to
examine the remains of the livery forge. Damn it,
he had no choice!

Not so Sam McAndrew. Sam had all the choices
in Creation. He could have ridden out of the hell-
hole any time he chose, and not a soul would have
raised a voice to stop him. Sam had taken all a
man could be reasonably expected to swallow.

So who would deny him the chance of a new life
almost anywhere he chose? The one-time town of
Grateful had turned its back on him once, might
it not again?

'No, Gus, that won't never happen,' Sam had

said, wincing as Doc Lesters dressed his shoulder
wound yet again. 'Town's been to Hell and seen it.
Yuh don't go riskin' yuh neck on a second look.
There's too many dead, too many buried – and a
darn sight too much to do round here for wastin'
time on Hell-watchin'! No, I'm stayin', Gus,
wearin' this badge 'til I decide other.'

'Whoa now, hold up there,' Shelley had frowned
at Doc's side. 'Not so fast. I figure I might have a
say in this somewhere.'

'And how`d yuh reckon for that?' Sam had
asked.

'Well, seein' as how it was m'self who was there
for yuh when yuh took that spread of lead, and
seein' as how it was *my* cabin provided yuh refuge
when yuh most needed it, and seein' too as how it
was *my* Colt in *my* hand that settled Walt Pond,
I'm lookin' to yuh owin' me some.'

'Yeah, well, what yuh sayin' is true enough,
Shelley, but I ain't sure how I'm goin'—'

'And another thing, yuh been slippin' in and
outa my sheets for too darned long, Sam
McAndrew. Treatin' my bed like it was some two-
bit livery where the stablin' comes free and the
feed along of it!'

'Now that ain't so,' blustered Sam through
another wince. 'I ain't never once—'

'And yuh ain't gettin' no younger neither. Not
by a half yuh ain't. So I'm sayin' as how we're
goin' to get ourselves wed, put this whole business
'tween you and me on a proper footin', just as soon
as Charlie Catches brings me some new silky
sheets from back there in Denver.'

'Who's waitin' on silky sheets?' Sam had croaked.

'Now that,' Doc Lesters had murmured, tightening the dressing, 'never did happen in Rockdale!'

So maybe it would all come right given time, thought Gus, running a hand over the cold forge. Maybe there was a future at that.

Shifty Becks still had no mind for a dusty boardwalk. Dirt was dirt whichever way you came to it, and Shelley's Saloon was no place to go finding it. Leastways, not while he had a besom in his hands and a clear, fresh morning, just like was coming up, to wield it.

Damn it, he thought, pausing to gaze into the breaking glare of early sunlight, life was getting to be worth living again. Two months after the blaze and the new town was taking shape, new folk settling along of it. Come a year and a fellow might be hard put to spot the scars of that night.

Not that some didn't fail to look. Sure, there were plenty of them.

Curious drifters, folk willing to hang on every word of how the O'Mara boys had died here, how Wino Keets and Casey Brett came to their miserable ends, how the story back East was that somebody, no names, no real description, slipped Sam McAndrew the Colt that finally settled Keets.

Well, mused Shifty, they could keep looking, keep asking, but his lips were sealed. Yessir, sealed good and tight, just like Miss Shelley had asked. And she was right, past was the past.

Nights ended and new days came up. And, God willing, they always would.

And, in any case, just like he had told them nosy drifters only yesterday, he had never heard of a place called Grateful.

This town went by the name of McAndrew.